READER PRAISE FOR 1

"I love this series. Kiru T. favorite authors. I think eve ...ies. The 3 friends are very hard not to love." ~ Amazon Reviewer

"I loved it. The way he loved her, strong chemistry between them. This is a great series 💜 🍦 beautiful." ~ Amazon Reviewer

"I truly enjoyed every book in this series and I can't wait to read more from this author." ~ Amazon Reviewer

ALSO BY KIRU TAYE

The Essien Series
Keeping Secrets
Making Scandal
Riding Rebel
Kola
A Very Essien Christmas
Freddie Entangled
Freddie Untangled

Bound Series
Bound to Fate
Bound to Ransom
Bound to Passion
Bound to Favor
Bound to Liberty

The Challenge Series
Valentine
Engaged
Worthy
Captive

The Ben & Selina Trilogy
Scars
Secrets
Scores

Men of Valor Series
His Treasure
His Strength

His Princess

Yadili Series
Duke: Prince of Hearts
Killer of Kings
Bad Santa
Rough Diamond
Tough Alliance

Royal House of Saene Series
His Captive Princess
The Tainted Prince
The Future King
Saving Her Guard
Screwdriver

Viva City FC Series
Tapping Up
Against the Run of Play

Others
Haunted
Outcast
Sacrifice
Black Soul
Scar's Redemption

Kiru Taye

First Published in Great Britain in 2021 by
LOVE AFRICA PRESS
103 Reaver House, 12 East Street, Epsom KT17 1HX
www.loveafricapress.com

Home of African Love Stories

Text copyright © Kiru Taye, 2016

ISBN: 978-1-914226-57-1
Also available in eBook

Blurb

Some secrets bind you...

Tessa Obum and her best friend, Anuli, are linked by a dark secret that could destroy them if it ever comes to light. Men are just the means to an end, and society shuns women like her. But she's determined to live on her terms and own her future. Until an encounter with the intense Peter has her questioning her choices.

Some challenges can break you...

Peter Oranye has never had a challenge he couldn't conquer. Except the death that claimed the only woman he loved. He's been unable to get close to another woman since, and his life is focused on growing his business empire. Until Tessa, a sexy bombshell of a woman, tumbles into him one night and he's ready to break his abstinence streak.

Getting involved with a woman who won't let go of her BFF is wrought with dangers, especially when someone else wants to destroy them. When their secrets come to light, will any of them be worthy of the love they crave?

Worthy

Dedication

To Sola,
You hounded me for months, until I finally wrote this
story.

Chapter One

Sometimes, you have to do wrong, to do right. ~
Tessa Obum.

"Grab those free seats and I'll get the drinks."

Tessa made a beeline for the only available table
in the already crowded nightclub while her friend
Anuli sauntered to the bar. She settled on one of the
low, padded oxblood chairs, pulling the other one
beside her and placing her purse on the cushion to
secure it so no one else carried it away as was likely
to happen.

They liked to get here early on a Friday night so
they would have enough time to relax and survey
potential marks. An accident on the road into Port
Harcourt had caused tailbacks, delaying them
tonight. In the end, they'd exited the taxi car and
flagged down motorbike riders instead. The bikers
had been able to navigate the traffic and take an
alternative route. To make sure no one saw them
arriving, they'd hopped off a street away and paid
the men.

Her gaze swept through the area. Xtasy was one
of the premier night spots in Port Harcourt. The
rich and the beautiful of the city came here. Dark

walls, dim lighting, low tables and dance music contributed to the party atmosphere. Bodies gyrated against each other on the dance floor. The music was loud but not enough to drown everything out. Smartly dressed people stood, chatting and holding colourful drinks in their hands.

A few tables from her, a man sat next to a woman who had to be his girlfriend from the way she draped over him. He kept glancing at Tessa, flipping his tongue over his bottom lip in a suggestive manner.

Tessa resisted rolling her eyes heavenwards and ignored him. The place was busy enough she didn't need to resort to some guy who should be paying attention to the woman next to him. She didn't roll like that.

Anuli manoeuvred through the crowd, carrying the bottles of Coke with the black straws sticking out of them. She plonked the drinks on the table as Tessa pulled her purse from the other seat, giving her room to sit.

One of their rules. They never drank alcohol unless someone else was buying it. The non-alcoholic beverages in here were expensive enough.

"Seen anyone interesting?" Anuli asked as she leaned back the seat and glanced around the space.

Tessa grabbed her drink. "No one specific—" She leaned towards her friend, so no one else would overhear. "—but the guy in the red shirt at the table to my right has been eyeing me."

Anuli tilted her head as she picked up her drink. "You mean him with the girl in purple?"

"That's the one." Tessa rolled her eyes.

"Na wa for some people. No be babe dey with am?" Anuli replied in the local Pidgin English which they used privately for conversations.

"Are you telling me?" There was nothing more annoying than a man with a beautiful woman who was still ogling every other woman in the room.

She had a rule. They both did. They never encroached on another woman's territory. If a man was so obviously taken, then they avoided him. Men with other women and men wearing wedding bands were off limits.

Of course, some married men came here, hoping to pick up single women. If he didn't wear a ring and didn't declare himself as with someone else, then he was fair game.

"Well, let's give him something interesting to look at." Anuli nudged forward and planted her lips on Tessa's, giving her a brief kiss.

The man's eyes went wide, and his body racked as he coughed.

"It looks like you just gave the idiot a heart attack," Tessa said with a giggle.

Anuli glanced over and laughed. "That'll teach him."

"Troublemaker." Tessa smiled. Her friend had always been bold and uninhibited. Over the years of their friendship, Tessa had learned to be free and adventurous too. There was no other way to the life they lived. Their exploits had been born out of necessity, a need to survive rather than a search for thrills. The excitement was just the by-product. "Now I have to go and reapply my lipstick. I'm coming."

She stood and headed to the ladies', weaving through the throng of people. The smell of perfume and cologne mixed with smoke and sweat in the warm air. There was always a good group of people out here on Friday night—wealthy men, white expatriates—all looking to have fun. All with money to burn.

Tessa and Anuli were here to help them blow the dough. They were working girls with bills to pay.

As she came out of the bathroom stall, Tessa caught her reflection in the mirror. In the empty, muted space, she glanced at herself again. It was always a shock to see the transformation in her whenever she came out on Friday night. She looked like a different woman from the person she was during the day. During the week.

Now, another woman stared back at her with brown tresses of wavy clip-in extensions almost to her hips, smoky dark eyes and sultry red lips. The short-sleeved, soft stretch jersey dress moulded onto curves stopping mid-thigh, and her velvet platform shoes made her appear taller than her usual five-feet-eight height.

She stood unrecognisable. She preferred it this way. The person she was on these nights wasn't who she was for the rest of the time.

Keeping the two personalities, and worlds, separate was key to her survival.

What if you're discovered? A cold finger skittered down her back, and she shuddered, pushing the thought aside. She didn't want to entertain the terrible idea tonight or any other night.

She reapplied the ruby red lipstick before hurrying to the door. She needed to get back to the social atmosphere of the club. Friday nights weren't meant for gloomy self-introspections.

As soon as she stepped out of the door, she collided with someone. An unyielding rock of a person. The force of the impact sent her stumbling back on her stilettos.

"Oh," the man said and reached for her flailing arms.

Fingers wrapped around her upper arms and tugged. She slammed into the warmth of his compact abs. Breath whooshed out of her lungs, and she clutched his navy silk shirt to get steady.

For a moment, she didn't move. A little disorientated. A little sucked in by the safety of the body cocooning her. Something made her lean in, close her eyes and suck in a huge breath. A fresh, clean scent filled her nostrils.

Wow. He smelled good. Better than good. Divine. She couldn't remember the last time she stood this close to a man who made her was to nuzzle him and mark her body with his scent of cranberry, lemon, sage and man.

He couldn't have been in the nightclub for long because the scent of sweat and smoke didn't linger on his clothes.

There was a smoking ban in enclosed spaces and a sealed designated smokers' section located in the club. But this late in the evening when everyone buzzed on alcohol and fun, people smoked in the main club area as the ban wasn't enforced strictly.

13

"Are you okay?" The sound of his voice rumbled low. It seemed to emanate from his chest.

Shivering, she opened her eyes and looked into his. Her breath caught. His were an obsidian shade, dark and compelling. His smooth skin was a tawny colour, the hair cut close to his scalp. Brown brows arched over alert eyes, sharp nose bridged a symmetrical face, completed by lush lips and a square chin.

She wasn't a small girl, and she stood in tower-high shoes. Still, he loomed over her. His navy dress shirt buttoned up without a tie. She followed the lean line across his wide shoulders down to the narrow hips and legs in charcoal trousers onto the ebony wingtips.

He was fucking hot—front cover of GQ magazine jalapeno hot.

Her body temperature went mercurial, and she wished for a blast of arctic air.

"Hello?" His voice rumbled with concern.

He'd asked if she was okay and she hadn't replied. Heat spread up from her chest, and she worked saliva into her dry mouth before speaking.

"Yes, I'm okay." Her voice sounded alien. "Thank you. Sorry. I'm not usually this clumsy."

She brushed fallen hair away from her cheek, a little shaken by her response to this man. This gorgeous man.

"It's fine. I was the one walking fast." He squeezed her arms as if trying to reassure her that it wasn't her fault. "I should've known someone could be coming out of the door. Let me buy you a drink to make up for it."

Releasing her, he stepped away.

A pang spread across her chest. She missed his closeness, his solidity. His warmth. There'd been something between them when their bodies touched, sparking in the air and sizzling along her nerve endings. She wanted to feel it again.

"How about you dance with me instead?" She stepped near him, hoping to re-establish physical contact.

Lines appeared on his forehead as he frowned and glanced towards the archway leading to the main club area. "I'm not a good dancer."

He looked back at her with those dark, assessing eyes of his. She looked great in her outfit and unless he already had female company which wasn't likely if he were offering to buy her a drink, then he hopefully wouldn't be able to resist her offer to dance.

Curling her lips in a slow, seductive smile, she traced her fingertips along his arm. "It's not that challenging, and I bet you're a man who can do whatever he puts his mind to."

He grinned, a boyish grin complete with a dimple that made him appear younger than the early to mid-thirties she'd placed his age.

"When you put it that way, I can certainly try."

"Great." She ran her tongue over the inside tip of her bottom lip, tasting the lipstick. "I'm Tessa."

"Peter," he said as she pulled him along onto the dance floor.

The music playing was 'Yes No' by Banky W, a slow rhythm that made her step close to him and clasp his shoulders. They stood inches apart.

"Sway with me," she said and started moving.

He hesitated only for a few heartbeats before he moved with her, wrapping his arms around her back and pulling her even closer, so their bodies met, hips to hips. He danced with ease. Fluidly. Expertly.

Humility. A rare quality among Nigerian men. She'd met so many who'd proudly boasted about being great on the dance floor or in bed for that matter and still failed to deliver.

This man, Peter, exceeded her expectations within minutes of meeting her.

Her entire body thrummed, the spark of something between them reigniting. She tilted her head, sweeping the hair away from her face. Her pulse picked up speed. Adrenaline rushed through her veins. Leaning close to his ear, she spoke so he could hear her. "You're good at this. What were you worried about?"

"I haven't done this in a long time." There was a sigh in his voice, a hint of regret that called to her in a way no other man had ever done.

His breath whispered against the skin of her nape. A tingle raced down her spine, and she almost moaned out loud. Their entwined bodies flowed with ease across the dance floor.

She'd always known that music could have erotic cadence, and she'd used it in the past to entrap others. She got lost in the motion, no longer the one in control of the situation.

Not with the snug way Peter held her in the security of his body. Not with her head cradled on his shoulders and her mind focused on him. Not with the way her belly fluttered and goose bumps skittered across her skin.

Everyone else on the dance floor seemed so far away. On another planet. She orbited on planet Peter.

The music changed. A faster beat this time with a throbbing baseline that vibrated throughout the space and bounced off the walls. They didn't separate, and Peter didn't let go of her.

What are you doing? The small voice in her head nagged. *Don't get comfortable. You're not on a date. You're working.*

She sighed. She'd never been this relaxed in the company of a man before now. She'd almost forgotten the reason she was here and just gotten swept away in the moment. She needed to up the game.

When the track changed a third time, she twisted around, her back to his chest, her bum to his crotch. She rolled her hips, feeling the rock of his erection against the flimsy material of her dress. An answering arousal pooled between her legs, her insides contracting on emptiness.

Another first. She knew how to walk the talk. She'd played the game often enough; she'd mastered pretending to be aroused in male company. But actual arousal? The knickers-soaked kind that made her want to climb a man—this man—and ride his cock just for the pure pleasure of it? Nah. Never.

This had to be a fluke. Perhaps because Anuli had kissed her earlier and her body was already primed.

Peter gripped her with one arm around her stomach and the other holding onto her left hip.

"You're a naughty girl," he said in a gruff voice. The warm air from his breath fanned the column of her neck making it even more sensitive. She wished he would place his lips there, but he didn't.

"What are you going to do with me for being bad?" she asked. A warm shiver went down her spine at all the things they could get up to together.

He chuckled, a rich, warm sound which vibrated through her body. "We'll see."

She allowed her head to fall back onto his shoulder, one hand on his hip and the other on his arm. This had to be the most intimate dance she'd ever had in public.

Just having him hold her this way without doing anything overtly sexual was making her pussy clench tight repeatedly. She was close to an orgasm.

An orgasm. That would be something to experience considering no man had ever given her one before.

When she closed her eyes and pictured a head between her legs, tongue swirling around her clit, the chin had stubble grazing her thighs and the face in her mind was that of Peter's.

"Uh." She moaned out loud. She was in trouble and at risk of embarrassing herself out here. Perhaps it was time to seal this deal.

"Can we get out of here?" she asked as she turned around to face him.

He didn't say anything, his face a mask of intensity. What was he thinking? Would he walk away?

The ache in her chest caught her unawares. She shouldn't care. He was one man in a sea of plenty. She steeled her mind, ready for his rejection.

Instead, he nodded. "Come with me."

He took her hand, leading her off the dance floor towards the exit. Her heart raced, drumming in her chest. She glanced around the space to find Anuli and eventually found her chatting with a guy at the bar.

Tessa smiled to herself. She would send her friend a message to say she'd left.

Outside, fresh air cooled her hot skin, and she breathed easy. The night temperature had dropped a few degrees, and a slight sea breeze whipped the green and white flag on the building across the road. The road was chaotic with rivers of traffic and bustling pedestrians during the day. Now at close to midnight according to the phone she pulled out of her purse, the human and vehicular traffics reduced to trickles.

Instead of taking her to one of the cars in the parking lot, Peter strode across the tarmac, along the pavement and towards the brightly lit building next door.

Heart racing and palms sweaty, she stopped walking. "Are you staying here?"

This was a high-end hotel. People like her weren't permitted to stay, never mind that she couldn't afford their room rates.

Halting, he glanced at her, and something flickered in his eyes that she couldn't understand. Perhaps it was just the play of the light and shadow in the courtyard. "Yes, this is my residence for a few days."

With the sure way he carried himself and the fancy outfit he wore, he could certainly afford to pay for the hotel. It wasn't her expense to worry about, anyway.

Still, she didn't move as her muscles tensed. She bit her bottom lip and sucked in a gulp of air.

"Did you want me for the night or just a few hours?" She preferred to agree on the deal before she went with the client, so there wasn't any confusion about the fees later.

He scrubbed a hand over his face, frowning. "Let's see how it goes."

"Okay. It's just that the cost is ten thousand for the night. And I've got to send a message to my friend to tell her where I've gone."

His body went rigid, and he pulled his hand away from hers. "What? Ten thousand?"

"Yes, that's for the whole night but if you'd prefer an hourly rate..." She trailed off.

His mouth slackened, his eyes blinking rapidly. He seemed lost for words. She wondered if he was one of those miserly types. His clothes cost more than fifty times the amount.

"You're..." He scrubbed a hand on his head again. "A call girl?"

She flinched at the accusation in his voice. "Didn't you know?"

"Of course not!" He stared at her, but it was as if he didn't see her. Looking down, he shook his head before turning and walking away without looking back.

Shit. Her lungs constricted, making it hard to breathe.

Chapter Two

Lips pressed tight and body hunched over, Tessa didn't move for a few seconds after Peter walked away. She gulped in air to ease the constriction in her chest.

Why did she feel so disappointed? So hurt. It wasn't the first time a man had turned her down. And it wouldn't be the last.

So why did Peter's apparent disapproval and rejection sting more than any other she'd experienced before?

At the early days, she and Anuli had struggled with identifying locations where they could find men who would be willing to pay for sexual services. They hadn't wanted to walk the streets, instead selecting their targets from clubs and bars. In those days, it had been tough, and she'd had to grow a thick skin and keep her primary objective in mind. This was only ever going to be a means to an end. Not a lifetime career.

When Anuli had found out about this nightclub, they'd hit the jackpot. The men who frequented the place were always willing to spend the cash, especially for a night with a beautiful girl.

So, Peter's reaction, especially after the fun they'd had in the club, had been a punch to the gut.

The whooshing sounds of sliding doors made her look up towards the entrance to the hotel, expecting Peter to walk out. To say he didn't mean to leave her standing out here in the chilly night.

Instead, a man and woman holding hands walked inside the building.

She blew out a heavy sigh. It was silly of her to hope. What was she going to do now? Strangely, her stomach grew thick at the idea of going back to the nightclub. She couldn't go home. Not without earning some cash tonight.

Her phone beeped. She took a deep breath before unlocking it.

Where are you? A text message from Anuli.

I'm outside. I'm coming back in. She sent a reply and headed in the direction of the night club. There was no point moping around. There were other fishes in the sea. And she meant to catch one tonight.

The doorman let her back in. They had a good deal going on with him. He guaranteed their entrance into the nightclub by slipping him a thousand Naira note every time they came here. When they started visiting, he would point out the real high rollers for them, and they would tip him extra. It was a high taxation, but it ensured they earned money without harassment.

Inside, Tessa found Anuli seating in a cluster of chairs with two guys she introduced as Telema and David.

Probably in their late twenties or early thirties, they were dark-skinned and okay looking. Honestly, their looks didn't matter. On their nights working, the girls judged the men by two standards.

Were the men spending money freely? This was the first criterion. The girls were here to earn money and a man who parted with his cash readily was more likely to pay for sex than one who didn't.

Were the men acting like douche bags? Also important, as they'd found out that men who behaved like assholes were more trouble than they were worth.

Telema and David passed the first criterion. They ordered bottle after bottle of champagne. From the conversation, it seemed they'd sealed a big contract and were in a celebratory mode.

On the other hand, Tessa's douche bag meter appeared to be broken as she couldn't quite get into the party spirit. Although both men seemed charming enough, her initial enthusiasm from being at the club had fizzled away with Peter's departure.

"Is everything okay?" Anuli leaned close to her side. It seemed her friend noticed her lack of interest in the fun atmosphere.

"Sure." She forced a smile on her face. This wasn't the place to discuss what had happened with Peter. Not when she still had to get through the evening and earn the money she needed.

It shouldn't matter anyway. Peter was just some guy like any other guy in here. What she'd shared with him had been just a moment in time. It was gone now. No big deal. She needed to snap out of it.

"How about we take this party to a more private location, ladies?" David said it more like a statement than a question, with a huge grin on his face.

Tessa's skin prickled at having to tell the men the cost of spending the night with them. She'd never been shy about what she did, but her encounter with Peter left her feeling raw.

"Do they know the score?" she asked her friend in a small voice.

"Yes. I settled the deal already. Fifteen grand each for the night," Anuli replied with a wink and a smile.

The men were generous, which also put a smile on Tessa's face. Perhaps this night wouldn't be such a dud after all.

Still, her scalp prickled as she hung onto Telema's arm. He led her out of the venue and across the courtyard on the same route that Peter had taken. *Not again.*

"Are you staying at the hotel?" she asked, not wanting to go in there in case she bumped into Peter, which was ridiculous as the place was massive. What were the chances of the two of them meeting again? Minimal, right?

"Just for the night." The guy winked at her.

She realised he meant he was only staying there because he probably didn't want to take her home to his house. She glanced at his ring finger but didn't see any evidence that he was married. It didn't mean he wasn't.

Still, what did she care? She wanted the night to be over already. The sooner they got down to business, the sooner she could get out of here.

Inside, the foyer was well lit and modern—sleek surfaces and gleaming marble flooring. Everything glittered. The place was classy, and the management was strict about call girls in the premises. The doorman at the nightclub had warned them not to come here, ages ago.

There was a smaller, cheaper motel just down the road that they usually ended up in with clients who didn't want to take them back to their homes.

At the reception desk, the men arranged for the accommodation and within minutes they headed up to the rooms in the lift. David had his arm around Anuli's shoulders as they turned left on the first-floor corridor.

Telema led her to the right and opened a door with his key card. As soon as she stepped into the room, Peter crept back into her mind. Was he staying in one of the adjacent rooms? What if he heard them?

Don't be ridiculous, girl.

She gave herself a mental shake. Of course, he couldn't hear them. Even if he stayed next door and heard sounds, he wouldn't know who was in the room.

Telema shut the door behind her. "I saw you dancing tonight. You made me wish I was the one dancing with you. Now I have the chance. I want you to dance with me."

Tessa felt something twist in her gut. The dance with Peter had been special. She hadn't danced that way with anyone else before. So lost in the moment, she hadn't even been aware someone was watching them. Now she wasn't sure she could recreate the atmosphere, even if she recreated the moves.

"There's no music," she replied, looking around the clean room with a double bed, a table and chair and a door leading to the bathroom. Yep, this was above her price range.

Grinning, he reached into his pocket, pulled out his phone and fiddled with it until a song started playing. It was the same one from the night club.

She shook her head in disbelief that he would play the same track she'd been dancing to, and his grin only widened as he tugged her close.

"Come on, Tessa. Show me your moves."

She placed her hands on his shoulders as he wrapped his arms around her back, his hands on her butt.

Peter hadn't done that. He hadn't groped her or leered at her. Still, she'd been turned on in his presence.

Now, Telema felt all wrong. Smelled all wrong. He smelled of alcohol and sweat mixed with cologne. He wasn't as tall as Peter which meant she stood taller in her high heels. But Telema's body was bulkier like someone who spent a lot of time lifting weights in the gym.

His erection pressed against her hip as he moved in sync with the song, squeezing her bum cheeks. Instead of getting excited, nausea roiled her stomach. The fast way he held her made her want to wriggle away. Her breath locked in her chest as if he was suffocating her.

She couldn't help comparing the man to Peter. Dancing with Peter had been different. She'd been comfortable, secure and excited in his arms.

Now uneasiness made her move rigidly, and she swallowed excessively. She certainly wasn't aroused, although that didn't matter in the scheme of things. In situations like this, the client's pleasure was more important than hers. She was getting paid to please him.

Still, when the track changed, she shifted away from Telema in a hurry.

"We're not done yet," he said as another song came on and he pulled her back, this time turning her back to his chest, her bum to his crotch.

As soon as he pressed his lips on the bare skin of her shoulder, her body itched as if ants were crawling on her skin and she stepped away from him. "I can't do this. I'm sorry."

"What?" He reared back, looking surprised. Then a knowing smile curled his lips. "Do you want more money? I'll pay you an extra five thousand to give me the sexy dance."

He reached into his pocket and pulled out his wallet.

Twenty thousand Naira for a few hours with him? It was double what she would've charged Peter and would come in handy.

But this whole situation felt wrong. She couldn't put a finger on why except that she didn't want to dance with Telema. It was as if she was ruining the special moment she'd had with Peter. Silly, but there was no other way she could explain it.

"That's not what I mean. I don't want more money. I changed my mind about the whole deal," she said, meeting his gaze squarely so he would understand that she was serious.

He frowned. "You followed me up here. And now you want to change your mind? You can't do that." He took a step towards her, shoulders squared, eyes glaring, crowding her.

She backed away. Not wanting to turn her back to him, she reached behind, probing for the doorknob. "Yes, I can. You haven't paid me yet, so you haven't lost anything."

"I'm not going to lose anything because you're going to do whatever I say." His face was now an angry mask, and he grabbed her shoulder, twisting her towards the bed.

She wriggled in his hold, pushing to get away.

"Let go of me," she shouted, her mouth dried out.

The rip of her dress sounded like an omen as she shoved against him. Panic rose. Adrenaline rushed through her as her pulse pounded. She had to get away from him. He was bigger and stronger. If he got her onto the bed, she wouldn't be able to get away from him.

Raising her leg, she didn't have the space to knee him in the groin. So, she did the alternative and stamped on his foot as hard as she could with the spiked heel of her stiletto.

"Ouch!" he yelped and loosened his grip on her arms, bending over to grab his foot. "Bitch! You'll pay for this."

Tessa didn't wait to see what he would do. She rushed to the door, flicked the lock and yanked it open. She ran into the corridor and headed for the stairs, ignoring the lift because she didn't know how long it would take to arrive. She didn't want to be in the hallway when Telema came out.

Moving fast in the high heels proved tricky. At the top of the stairs, she paused to pull off her shoes and heard stomping footsteps on the carpet behind her. Glancing back, she saw Telema hobbling quickly in her direction, his expression murderous.

She tugged her heels off and raced down the stairs. At the bottom, she rushed across the lobby, trying not to draw attention to herself from the receptionist or the man standing guard at the door.

"Stop that girl!"

Tessa froze and glanced back only to find an angry Telema at the bottom of the stairs, pointing a finger as he walked in her direction. She gave a quick look at the male receptionist and the doorman. They both stood at alert now as they finally noticed her.

Shit! There was no way she was going to get past the security man, and the receptionist looked ready to apprehend her. How was she going to get out of this jam?

"Sir, what's the matter?" the receptionist asked.

Telema stomped over and grabbed Tessa's arm, dragging her to the desk while she tugged her arm to get free.

"This girl stole my money," he said.

"What?" She twisted, glaring at him. "That's a lie. I didn't touch your money."

With pursed lips, he cocked his head as if saying 'who's going to believe you over me?'

He would be correct. In this kind of situations, people would tend to believe the richer-looking person. He was the hotel guest and appeared well-off in his expensive clothes. On the other hand, she was a call girl caught running out of the hotel. She looked guilty. Not to mention she was standing barefooted, her dress torn, her hair in disarray with her shoes and bag in her hand.

"I'm going to call the manager," the receptionist said and picked up the phone as he looked dubiously from Tessa to Telema.

Oh God! Her night was about to go from bad to worse. What would the manager do? Perhaps get the police involved if Telema persisted with his story. The police would lock her up without question. Things would be a whole lot worse than whatever Telema had planned for them in his room.

She couldn't be arrested, couldn't allow people to know what she did for a living.

She lowered her voice so only Telema could hear. "Why are you doing this? I didn't steal your money."

He tugged her arm, leading her away from the desk.

"I warned you wouldn't get away with it," he said through gritted teeth.

"Look," she said, still annoyed. Why was he so nasty because she didn't want to have sex with him? "You were trying to force me, and I panicked and kicked you."

His expression darkened, his nostrils flared.

Men and their fragile egos. She stopped from rolling her eyes in disdain. No need making him angrier. She needed to massage his ego so he'd calm down.

She sucked in a deep breath, counted to five silently and puffed it out. "I'm sorry. Okay? Please tell them I didn't steal your money."

"If you want me to forget about it, then you should come back upstairs with me. I know how you can make it up to me."

He gave her a lecherous grin which only made her stomach congeal and her skin itch. She couldn't stand him. Not after witnessing him trying to force her. What was she going to do? She didn't want to be anywhere near Telema. Still, she couldn't imagine what the hotel management would do with her.

What kind of shit was this?

She knew from first-hand experience that if a man showed any sign of violence once against a woman, then there was high likelihood he would repeat that offence, even when they apologised about the first time.

Telema had already shown his hand by rough handling her in the room. If she went back there, then she might as well be prepared to die. He would use aggression again.

She would never willingly give a man the chance to brutalise her once more.

"Tessa?"

At the sound of her name, she stiffened and a cold shiver travelled down her spine. She recognised the rumbling voice instantly. The deep cadence was imprinted in her mind and conjured up an image of two bodies writhing on the dance floor.

Oh God. Please, not him. Not now. She prayed it was just her mind playing tricks on her and glanced in the direction of the voice.

Peter strode towards the middle of the lobby from the bar lounge, which was on the opposite side of the reception desk. He was dressed in the same outfit as earlier, except his shirt was undone at the top two buttons, his sleeves rolled up his arms to his elbows, and he had a smart phone in his right hand.

He stopped only a few feet from her and Telema. The curl of his lips and wrinkling of his nose registered his disapproval.

Burning rose from her chest to her face. She wished the floor would open and swallow her.

Her night had turned into a nightmare.

Chapter Three

Peter stood in the hotel lobby, muscles tense and quivering. He'd been on his way up to his suite after having a night cap at the bar when the commotion at the reception desk had drawn his attention.

Shoving his hands into his front trouser pockets, he glared at Tessa. What the hell was she doing in here?

The question seemed to have an obvious answer considering what she did for a living and the fact a man stood next to her, holding onto her arm.

Finding out she worked as a hooker had been a kick in the gut. All the time they'd been together in the club, the way she'd moulded onto him as they'd danced, it had all been a trap. He'd been a mark—a job to her.

He didn't like being set up. Had she engineered it so by bumping into him?

He'd been on his way out of the night club when she'd tumbled into him—a bombshell wrapped in a stretchy black dress which did little to hide her dark, pliant, curvaceous body and tottering on high heels that screamed 'bend me over and fuck me.'

To keep her upright, he'd reached for her. The moment he'd pulled her against his body, there'd been a spontaneous link between them. She'd melded against him, relaxing in his hold. Instinctively, he'd grasped her as if she'd belonged in his arms.

In those seconds, he'd been transported to another time and place with another woman. He hadn't held a woman close in years, a lifetime ago it seemed.

He'd heard Tessa sniff his skin and sigh with pleasure. A smile had curled his lips at her response and he'd wanted to take her away to a quiet corner so he could find out more about her. So, he could get lost in her feminine wonder.

When she'd looked up at him, the yearning in the depths of her amber gaze had burned into him, sparking a hidden lust to life. A craving he'd thought long dead.

Adrenaline spiked, his legs weakened. He'd offered to buy Tessa a drink, deciding he wasn't in a rush to get back to the solitude of his suite after all. Telling her to come with him so they could talk in the hotel would have been presumptuous.

When she'd asked him to dance, a rush of pleasure had made his heart thud fast at the chance of being physically close to her again.

On the parquet floor, she'd set the blood in his veins alight, the low spark of attraction turning into a wild blaze. For the first time in a long time, in years, he'd found a woman physically irresistible. The way she moved against him. The smooth texture of her mocha skin. The soft bundle of her curves. The sound of her laughter. The blaze of need in her eyes. Everything about her had turned him on.

So, when she'd asked if they should get out of there, his normal, disciplined brain hadn't been functioning. Her bold and direct approach had pushed his buttons. Without much thought, he'd taken her hand and they'd walked out of night club.

His intention had been to bring her here and up to his suite. He'd wanted to get to know her without the loud music and gyrating bodies as distractions. He hadn't wanted to let her go. Not yet.

Until she'd started talking about money and the realisation of what she was had punched him right between the eyeballs.

A call girl? Yes, sex had been on his mind when he strode down the sidewalk with her hand in his.

The idea of paying for sex, of having sex for the first time in years with a hooker, had made his stomach roil and his skin had prickled with unease.

Still, when he'd looked at her, he hadn't seen a woman of ill-repute to be reviled. Instead, he'd seen a hot babe who made his dick as rigid as an iron rod. A sexy woman he'd wanted to lock up in his suite, spread out on his bed and fuck nine ways to Sunday until they were both boneless.

The conflict between how he felt for her job versus how he felt about her had been too much to get his head around. He'd just turned and walked away from her.

Now she stood here. In the hotel lobby. Barely more than two hours after Peter had been with her. With another man. Had they had sex already? Had the man paid to do whatever he wanted to her body?

She looked like they'd gotten up to something rough considering she had her shoes in her hand. The shoulder seam of her dress hung loose where it'd been ripped and her hair stood in disarray.

His gut wrenched at the idea that the man had touched her in any way. Pulling his hands out of his pockets, his knuckles cracked as his hands bunched into fists.

"What are you doing here?" he asked in a cold and sharp voice.

"P—Peter—I..." she stammered before trailing off and biting her bottom lip, her eyes cast down.

The man standing next to her gave Peter the once over. "Mister, this is none of your business."

Before Peter could respond, the manager of the hotel hurried out from the staff entrance into the foyer.

"What's the problem?" he asked the group gathered around the counter.

"This man said the girl stole some of his money," the receptionist replied, pointing at Tessa and the man.

The muscles on Peter's back tensed as nausea lurched in his gut.

Tessa was a hooker and thief? Damn! All her external beauty hid a devious personality.

He certainly didn't want to get involved now. Shouldn't get involved. Yet, he couldn't turn around. Couldn't bring his legs to move.

"Is this true, sir?" the manager asked.

"Yes. I'm Telema George. And this girl stole money from my room."

Peter recognised the George surname. They were a prominent family in Rivers State. So, it was perfectly likely girls would flock to him and perhaps try to get as much money out of him as possible.

"I'm sorry, Mr George. We have zero tolerance for thieves in this hotel. I'm going to call the police," the manager said and picked up the phone handset on the desk.

The manager was doing the right thing, following protocol. Thieves shouldn't be tolerated. They should be made to pay for their crimes. If Tessa thought she could steal from people in this hotel and get away with it, then she was in for a shock. Had she been planning to steal from Peter too, if he'd taken her to his suite?

Peter's gut clenched as if he'd been kicked, his body heavy with disappointment. For one brief, soppy moment tonight, he'd dared to think he would find delight in a woman's company. In Tessa's company. How wrong had he been? He dropped his head and closed his eyes, rubbing the bridge of his nose. Nothing else to do but walk away.

"Peter, please help me." Tessa's voice shook.

Peter lifted his head, stared at her and wondered what she wanted him to do.

Her eyes were over-bright and feverish, her gaze darting around the space. She rocked in place.

He recognised the desperation evident in her agitated motions. A chunk of his hardened heart crumbled. He swallowed to shift the lump in his throat. "Why should I help you?"

"I didn't steal his money. I swear it." There was a shimmer of tears in her eyes.

For some idiotic reason that he couldn't understand, he believed her. Fool that he was. He'd always been a sucker for a woman's tears. He had two younger sisters who'd maximised its effects often enough.

"Call the police," the man beside her said, sounding irritated.

The manager stared at Peter, phone in hand, waiting for his authorisation.

Puffing out a deep breath, Peter shook his head. "Christopher, hold off on calling the police for now. I'll let you know if things change."

The man with Tessa swivelled and glared at Peter. "Who the hell are you to get involved in something that doesn't concern you?"

Peter drew in an easy breath and relaxed his muscles. Shoulders back, chest out, he stared at the man with an unwavering steel, cold gaze. "Mr. George, my name is Peter Oranye and I'm the owner of Park Hotel."

Technically, he had one-third ownership considering his friends Michael Ede and Paul Arinze owned a third each of the shares. But right here right now, he had sole responsibility for the outcome of this situation.

"So, you see, everything that happens in this premises is my concern," he continued.

Tessa's mouth dropped open and her eyes went wide.

"Oh, I didn't know that. It's nice to meet you, Peter." The other man grinned. "I—"

"You may address me as Mr. Oranye," Peter cut him down. He couldn't stand the man especially for having anything to do with Tessa. He had an unexplainable hatred for any man Tessa had sex with. He was better off not coming across them. And seeing this one just turned his stomach. So, there was no way he was going to get on first name basis with him.

The grin on Telema's face disappeared and he jerked back as if affronted. Peter didn't care.

"Christopher, I'm going to use your office to have a chat with Mr. George and Miss Tessa, so we can resolve this situation," Peter continued.

"Of course, sir," the manager said and headed towards a door marked 'Staff Only'.

"Please follow him and we'll get this sorted in private," Peter said, waving a hand in the direction Christopher headed.

Although this was late on Friday night and there were only a few patrons still up and about, he didn't like having anything controversial being discussed out in the open. This was still a reputable business and he wanted to maintain the hotel's unblemished record.

Telema nodded and followed Christopher. Tessa hesitated for a moment before looking up at Peter and meeting his gaze. She fidgeted with the handle of her bag, blinked rapidly, opened her mouth and closed it as if unable to form words. The foyer lay cool from the AC but a sheen of sweat glistened on her skin.

The bold girl he'd met in the club seemed replaced by a frightened Tessa.

He resisted taking a step towards her. He wanted to reassure her that she would get a fair hearing. But he also didn't want her to think she could get away with causing trouble in his hotel.

If she wanted to sell her body, then it was her prerogative. But she couldn't do it in his premises ever again.

"Tessa, go on," he said, keeping his tone neutral.

Her throat rippled as she swallowed hard. She nodded and joined the other men down the corridor. Peter walked behind her, keeping a couple of strides between them. Her shoulders were slouched and her steps hesitant, her bag clutched to her side, shoes still in hand.

Why would she be reluctant about facing the other men if she was innocent of the accusation of theft? She was a woman who made money in the company of men. He expected her to be confident and relaxed like she'd been in the club. Perhaps she knew she was in trouble regardless of the stealing charges.

Christopher unlocked the door and allowed Telema to go in first. Tessa glanced at Peter before walking in.

Peter drew in a long breath, blew it out and followed suit. It had been a long day. He'd been hoping to get to bed soon. It looked like sleep was a long way off for him tonight.

"Thank you, Christopher. You can leave us alone."

"Yes, sir." The manager shut the door of the office on the way out.

Peter strode around the beech wood desk and settled into the blue cushioned office armchair. He waved at the matching chairs on the other side of the desk. "Please sit down, both of you."

Telema moved first, taking the one on Peter's left. Tessa walked slowly to the other seat and lowered her body into it. With her shoes and bag on her lap, her bum on the edge, she appeared as if she expected to sprint out of the room in the blink of an eye.

"Mr. George, tell me what happened." Peter leaned back in his chair, projecting calm that he didn't exactly feel. But he had to be neutral until he had heard both accounts. He would listen to the plaintiff first before turning to the defendant.

"Well, I met this girl—" the man started.

"Her name is Tessa. I'm sure you know that already." Peter interrupted him. The man was being rude by referring to Tessa as 'this girl' and Peter had no problems putting him in his place.

He couldn't stand the hypocrisy of the man. And people like him. If she was good enough for sex, then she should be good enough to be given basic courtesy.

"Of course, I know that," Telema said in an irritated voice. "Yes, I met Tessa at the night club and I brought her here to my room for us to continue having a good time. When I went into the bathroom, she took money from my wallet."

Tessa gasped, mouth falling open as her hand flew to her chest.

Telema's eyes flicked to the side but he ignored her reaction and continued. "I saw her running away and chased her down the stairs to the lobby where I caught her. I want her punished. You must call the police."

"Of course, Mr. George. I'll get to the bottom of this and deal with the young lady as required."

Telema's story didn't ring true. On the face of it, it seemed plausible that things had happened the way he narrated it. But it didn't explain why Tessa's outfit was torn and her hair in a mess.

Now was a good time to hear her version. He turned to her. "Tessa, tell me what happened. You met Mr. George at Xtasy, is that correct?"

"Yes...Sir. Um." She swallowed and wiped a hand over her mouth. "After...I went back into the club and met my friend Anuli. She was with Telema...Mr. George and another man whose name is David. They were buying us drinks and then eventually they suggested we come over here. They booked a room each. Anuli had already agreed the price with them." She swallowed again and looked away as if uneasy saying more.

"So, you came to Park Hotel to have sex with Mr. George for money?" Peter asked, wanting her to confirm the purpose for their stay in the hotel so he didn't make assumptions.

Telema shifted in his chair, restless as he coughed.

Tessa glanced at Peter and he nodded to encourage her.

"Yes," she said, twisting the handle of the black bag. "Anuli went with David and Mr. George took

43

me to his room. Inside, he wanted me to dance with him. He was playing music from his phone and we danced for a while. But things didn't feel right and I didn't want to continue so I told him to stop but he refused. He offered me extra money to stay and I rejected it. I didn't want to have sex with him. He grabbed me and we struggled. That's how my dress got torn."

She tugged at the torn seam for emphasis. "Then I stamped on his foot to try and get away. He let me go and I ran out of the room. I took my shoes off when I got to the stairs and ran down. But when I got to the lobby, he shouted for the men to stop me and told them I stole from him. It is a lie. I never touched his money. He said if I went back to his room with him, he would forget everything. That was just before you showed up."

"Did he give you any money?" Peter asked, wanting to find out how far they had gotten, even as bile rose in his throat. Why did the idea of another man touching her rile him so much?

In this moment, he envied judges who decided over criminal or civil cases, trying to make impartial decisions based on evidence without personal prejudices slipping in. In this matter, he had to decide based on their explanations, body language, very little evidence and his gut feeling.

"No. He never gave me any cash because we never had sex. I couldn't..." she trailed off.

Peter couldn't explain the rush of relief that went through him because she hadn't had sex with Telema. He tamped down the urge to walk round the table, pull her into his arms and kiss her. Crazy, but true.

"Mr. George. How much money do you say Tessa stole from you?"

Telema shrugged his shoulders. "I don't know exactly but I think it was Twenty Thousand Naira."

Tessa gasped again and shook her head.

Peter ignored her reaction and spoke in a calm tone. "So, if I search her bag, I should find the amount in there."

"I don't know. Anyway, why are we wasting time with all this? You should call the police already."

"I can't call the police until I'm sure that a crime has been committed. It would be wrong to accuse someone falsely."

"What? You think I'm lying? You're going to believe her over me? She's just a prostitute."

Peter's hands gripped the arms of the chair tightly but he still didn't raise his voice. "And you're a man who pays women for sex. You are no better than her in my opinion."

Telema pushed back his chair and stood. "You can't insult me like that. I'm Telema George."

Peter rose too, folding his hands across his puffed-out chest. "I know exactly who you are, Mr. George. You brought a call girl into my hotel against our policy. When the girl refused to have sex, you tried to force her. When that didn't work, you accused her of stealing. Attempted rape is a crime, Mr. George. Worse than theft."

"You can't prove anything." Telema sneered at him.

"In the same way you can't prove that she stole from you. Pass me your bag, Tessa."

She handed him the item without hesitation, her unease gone.

Placing the purse on the table, he unclipped the metal clasp and opened it wide. He removed the items, placing each on the table surface side by side as if he were baring her life to their eyes—a small brown tube of lipstick, a face powder compact of the same colour, a black butterfly hair clip, an aluminium ring with two house keys, a black mobile phone, a white pack of three female condoms, two strawberry flavoured condoms, a little pack of wet wipes and a small plastic bottle of lubricant.

These were the tools of her trade. They defined her in much the same way as the items in his briefcase defined him as a businessman. He learnt a lot about her from the contents of her purse.

Tessa was a woman whose appearance mattered and she understood the important of her sexual health. The constriction around his chest eased a little because she was smart enough to take precautions.

Telema leaned his hands on the top of the chair he'd vacated while Tessa watched on in silence, her arms around her midriff.

In the side pocket, he pulled out a bunch of used notes. He counted them out loud for everyone's benefit. Four Thousand and Five Hundred Naira. He tipped the bag over, shaking it. Nothing else came out. He dropped the empty purse on the desk.

"As you can see, Mr. George, Tessa doesn't have your money. If you paid her for the night, she should have at least ten thousand." He remembered how much she'd told him about her fee. "And you claim she stole twenty. But this is nowhere near that amount. How do you explain it?"

"I—I—I don't know. She could've hidden it somewhere. Have you searched her body? Who knows where women hide things?" he replied in a condescending tone.

"I didn't take your money. You can search me." She stood up abruptly, arms dangling down her sides.

"No one is going to conduct a body examination on you," Peter cut in, surprised at the vehemence in his tone. His muscles tightened. He couldn't explain this compulsion to protect her. But he'd be damned if he'd allow Telema or anyone else to probe her physically.

"She could be hiding the money anywhere," Telema grumbled, waving his hand up and down to indicate Tessa's person.

"I don't mind," Tessa quipped, hands akimbo as she glared at the man. Some of the sureness she'd exuded in Xtasy had returned.

"I do," Peter said in a firm voice, ending any argument. She might not mind having others poke and prod her, but it wouldn't happen under his watch. Not in his hotel, damn it. "There's barely enough material to cover your body in *that* dress, let alone hide twenty grand in Naira notes. I can see this without having you patted down." *Or stripped.* "I believe you didn't take Mr. George's money."

"What? You're going to believe her? Is this how you treat your hotel guests?" Telema straightened, nostrils flaring.

"Our respectable guests know better than to bring call girls here." Peter leaned his palms flat on top of the polished wood desk, intent on shutting this guy down once and for all.

He had so many reasons to dislike Telema. Arrogance. Hypocrisy. Dishonesty. Of all the faults, he hated liars the most. Couldn't stand them.

At least Tessa had been truthful as far as he could deduce from their interactions.

Telema glared, huffed and stomped towards the door. "I won't let this matter drop."

"Then I'm sure the press will be interested to know that the son of Chief Godwin George gets his kicks by raping hookers."

He swivelled, eyes bulging. "I didn't touch her!"

Peter rolled his shoulders nonchalantly. He hadn't attained so much success in his business endeavours without shades of ruthlessness "Same way she didn't steal your money, but it didn't stop you from accusing her falsely, did it?"

Telema deflated, his shoulders slumping. "Fine. I'll drop the accusation as long as you don't get the media involved."

"Fair enough," Peter said. He'd known playing the parent card would work. Mr. George Senior was well known in political circles. A scandal like the one his son courted wouldn't be good for him.

Telema nodded and opened the door.

"One last thing, Mr. George."

"Yes?"

"Next time you want to book a room for the night, use the hotel down the road. They won't mind your kind of night-time activities."

Telema glowered, his face puffed up ready to explode. He stomped out of the room, slamming the door.

Peter and Tessa stood staring at each other in silence, separated by the desk. The air hung heavy between them.

Her mouth dropped open, fingers touching the parted lips. She remained frozen, a deer caught in bright headlights, unsure of what to do next. He hadn't exactly planned what to do either after he'd gotten rid of Telema. *Let her go.*

"Thank...thank you, sir," she said in a soft, halting voice that called to a part of him that had lain dormant for so long.

Need tightened his gut, tendrils of warmth spreading across his flesh. Sensations he hadn't felt in years flared inside him for the second time tonight. He remembered the suppleness of her skin as he'd held her on the dance floor. *Damn.*

He lowered his body into the chair he'd vacated, hiding his blooming erection as he fought the urge to demolish the space between them and re-establish physical contact. To throw caution to the wind, raid the office safe for cash and toss them at her so he could bend her over this desk and sate his maddening lust.

Perhaps his years of celibacy had been a bad idea. Perhaps this was his body's way of protesting at his refusal to indulge in the pleasures of a woman's body for so long. The calm composure he wore as a trademark stood at risk of been shredded by this irresistibly sexy woman.

Chapter Four

Tessa's heart raced and her breath stalled. The wonder of the moment made her weightless, floating on a sea of amazement.

Peter had helped her. He'd believed her claim that she hadn't taken Telema's money. He'd sided with her and shown the other man up for the liar he was.

How was that possible? When had a man ever picked her over another? When had a man ever protected her? This kind of thing just didn't happen in her life.

After the way Peter had stalked off and abandoned her on the pavement earlier tonight, she'd thought he'd just been going through the motions when he'd ushered them into the privacy of the office. She'd been certain he would've instructed the manager of the hotel to call the police.

Cold sweat had drenched her skin at the idea of being locked up, adding to the shame scorching her cheeks and chest because Peter had witnessed her in this dishevelled state.

She'd been unable to meet his gaze when he'd arrived. But desperation had driven her to ask for his help. She hadn't known if he would help, especially after she'd seen the way his lips drew tight in seeming disappointment.

Now she stood in the office across from him, free of Telema and his accusation. Adrenaline coursed through her veins. She fought the urge to climb the desk so she could reach Peter and give him a hug of gratitude.

The silent, intent expression on his face made her think it wouldn't be welcome. His potent aura demanded attention without being intimidating.

With his unbuttoned shirt revealing tawny skin and his sleeves rolled up his arms, he seemed less like the disciplined, idealistic man whose disappointment had crushed her and more like the easy-going, sensual man whose body had promised so much pleasure while they'd been in Xtasy nightclub.

Her breathing became shallow. The sound of rushing blood filled her ears.

She couldn't look away from him, the awareness of him buzzing along her nerve endings. His presence translated into energy, a life-form stretching and undulating in the space around her, permeating her flesh. Desire flared in her belly. Her core clenched.

She closed her eyes briefly and sucked in a deep breath. His scent, clean and fresh, filled her lungs and she was transported back to the dark club, the throbbing music and their entangled bodies on the dance floor, his cocooning hers in warmth.

Her pussy clenched and she suppressed a moan, popping her eyes open.

His dark gaze pierced hers and she swallowed to get her mouth working. She had to say something.

"Thank you, sir." Her voice sounded low; she wasn't sure if he heard her.

"What are you thanking me for?" he asked, his expression still unreadable.

Jeez, he made her self-conscious. Out of her depth. Men usually didn't intimidate her. Not when she was dressed to kill. Dressed to seduce. As vampy Tessa, she stood confident, conqueror of men's libidos. Ruler of her life.

With one look, Peter unravelled her. He'd done something to her tonight. When he'd walked away from her, she'd lost something. *Her edge.* It was the only way she could explain the debacle with Telema afterwards. On any normal Friday night, she would've had Telema eating out of her hands.

Instead, she stood in this office, barefooted and dishevelled, her composure rattled.

Avoiding his gaze and needing to do something to distract from the thoughts in her head, she picked up her bag and started putting the items Peter had taken out and left on the table back into it.

"For helping me even when you didn't necessarily believe me." She gave him a surreptitious glance from the corners of her eyes.

His shoulders lifted and fell in a fluid, languid motion. "Getting the police involved wouldn't have been good for the hotel. I had that to consider."

"Oh." She swallowed hard, disappointment making her lower her head as she sat back in the chair. There she'd been thinking he'd done it for her. Instead, he'd been trying to save the image of his hotel. It made sense. He didn't know her, so why should he do anything for her. Still...

"So, you really own this hotel." She waved her hand to encompass the space, trying to exude coolness. She had to forget how he affected her and just concentrate on the here and now, and what happens next.

"Yes, me and two of my friends." He picked up a blue biro and started writing on a notepad.

She wondered what he was writing and looked around the office—the manager's office—white walls, a lightwood desk with a computer and a mesh metal file tray, blue upholstered armchairs on wooden frames, a grey metal cabinet at the corner and navy carpets.

"You didn't tell me earlier that you owned the hotel." She glanced at him again.

He stared up at her briefly with assessing eyes as if trying to figure out why she asked the question and returned to what he was writing. "We didn't get the chance to talk."

She shifted in her seat as her cheeks heated. When they'd met, he'd been keen to bring her to the hotel. She'd ruined their evening by revealing her job to him.

What else had she missed out of finding out about him? Would he have kissed her? Would he have given her the pleasure his body had promised on the dance floor? She'd never find out now.

Sighing, she picked up her bag, contents restored. It was best to just leave. "I should head off."

"No, you can't." He didn't look up, seemingly concentrating on what he was writing.

"Why?" There was no reason for her to be here and he appeared to be busy anyway.

Lifting his head, he dropped the pen and folded his lower arms on the desk. "Did you know you weren't allowed to come into this hotel with guests to ply your trade?"

Wincing, she fidgeted with the handle of her bag. "Yes, I knew this hotel was out of bounds."

"Yet, you still came here with your 'friends'." He air quoted the word 'friends.' "Any call girl caught on the premises is handed over to the police and detained. Did you know that?"

Sweat broke on her forehead, her pulse rate speeding up. She seemed to have jumped from frying pan into fire.

"Yes." She coughed. "I knew that."

"So, you know that I'm entitled to call the police."

"Y—yes." She shuffled her bare feet against the rough carpet.

"Good." He shoved his seat back and stood up. "Follow me."

Abandoning the notepad he'd been writing on, he strode past her towards the door.

Her palms turned clammy as she gripped the arms of the chair tight. She didn't move, unsure of what would happen. Was he going to call the law? Shit. She couldn't end up in jail.

Still sitting, she turned in his direction. "Peter, I'm sorry for all the inconvenience I caused you and the hotel today. I promise I won't come here again. Please don't hand me over to the police."

He tipped his head forward and leaned against the wall, his back to her for a few seconds. Was he struggling to decide? In the little time they'd spent together, his actions showed him to be a man of integrity. A just man.

She'd broken the rules by coming here and deserved to be punished. But getting the law involved would open a can of worms. She didn't want to go there. Not tonight. Not ever.

Turning, he met her pleading gaze with his composed one. "I'm not going to call the police...this time. But there's something you'll have to do."

Puffing out a breath, she stood and braced herself. "Whatever you want, I'll do it. Just not the police." Nothing could be as bad as the police.

"Okay." He breathed out. "Come on then. Put your shoes back on."

Tentatively, she did as he instructed and followed him out of the office as they headed down the narrow corridor. He walked ahead of her.

Rolling her tongue over her bottom lip, she admired the hug of his trousers over his butt and the powerful strides of his sturdy legs. He really was a striking man, front and back.

At the door to the lobby, he glanced at her as he held the slab open for her to walk through.

He'd caught her ogling his fine ass. Her cheeks heated. She really needed to get her head out of the gutter when it came to Peter. He wasn't interested in her like that regardless of what had happened in the night club.

"Tell Christopher I'll be in my suite if he needs me. I've left a note for him in the office," Peter said to the receptionist.

The area was back to its normal serene atmosphere with low jazz music coming from the bar lounge adjacent. There was no evidence of the earlier scuffle between her and Telema. The doorman only gave her a cursory glance and the receptionist seemed rapt on Peter.

"Yes, Sir," the man replied. "I'll let him know. Good night."

"Thank you, Kefre," Peter said before turning to Tessa. "This way."

Sweeping his hand, he ushered her towards the lift.

"Where are we going?" She didn't believe he would take her to his suite. It didn't make sense.

"You'll see." He pressed the button and they rode up in silence.

Being in an enclosed space with him made her pulse pound fast and the tightness in her chest loosened.

She took a sideways glance at him. He had his back to the wall and was staring straight ahead. He appeared calm. How could he be so composed when her heart was galloping and her palms were sweaty?

Didn't he feel this connection between them? It was so tangible she could cut it with a knife.

She barely controlled herself. Every fibre in her body wanted to get close to him. Wanted to have his hardness wrapped around her. Thrusting deep inside her.

The ping of the lift made her flinch.

He waited for her to exit the lift before he strode to one of the doors, inserted a key card, opened it and waved her inside.

Her breath caught as she entered the suite. The overhead lamp flicked on, bathing the space in muted orange light. She'd never seen a hotel room which looked like this. This wasn't a room. Telema had a nice room with a double bed and mod cons.

This was a swanky flat—a luxurious apartment. No other way to describe it. It was huge with separate living and sleeping areas as well as the bathroom she could see through the open door. The walls were an off-white shade, the furniture and furnishings in varying shades of brown.

"Is this part of the hotel?" she asked as she gawped at the place. It could've been his home from the looks of it.

Smiling, he shut the door and tossed his phone and keys on top of a side table. "Yes. It's one of the high-end suites. I stay here when I'm in Port Harcourt."

"It's amazing," She gushed but she had no shame about it. She'd been in a few hotels in the city but never seen any rooms like this one.

"Thanks. Make yourself comfortable. This is where you'll be staying for the night."

Every muscle in her body froze although her heart raced.

Peter wanted her to stay? Had he changed his mind about having sex with her? Did he want to pay her for the evening?

Her stomach fell, and bile rose in her throat. Why had she thought he stood apart from every other man who wanted to use her body? Worse, why did her chest hurt at the fact that he wasn't any different from the rest? She'd been stupid to place him on a pedestal just because he'd helped her with Telema.

All men were the same, and Peter was about to prove it.

"Are we...?" She couldn't bring herself to complete the question.

He leaned against the dining table, crossed his legs at the ankles and folded his arms over his chest.

"If you mean are we going to have sex tonight, Tessa? The answer is no. I didn't bring you here to pay you to pleasure me. I brought you here because I can't stand the thought of you going back to that night club and picking up another man who's going to do God-knows-what to you. I can't allow that."

Her mouth dropped open at his declaration. She couldn't believe what she just heard. She straightened up, placed one hand on her hip, the other gripping her bag, and lifted her chin.

"Hang on a minute. You brought me here so you could control me and prevent me from working? You have no right to do that."

He uncrossed his arms and took steps towards her, stopping a foot away. He rubbed a hand on the back of his neck, his jaw clenched, his neck muscles corded.

"You can get one thing straight. You're in my hotel. My rules apply. Only a few hours after I met you, you ended up in a room with another man in my hotel. He could've raped you. You could've been locked up in a police cell."

She balled her hands into fists and met his frustrated gaze with glaring eyes. She was back in her stilettos, so she was almost head-to-head with him.

She started doing this job because she didn't want a man to control her. She'd be damned if she would let Peter or anyone else tell her what she could or couldn't do.

"Look. I appreciate you helping me out. But this is my body." She jabbed her right thumb at her heaving cleavage. "I have the right to choose who I give it out to, when and where. It's my choice. Neither you nor anyone else can tell me what to do, damn it."

He leaned forward, his face only inches away from her and lowered his voice. "It might be your right to choose what you do to your body. But for tonight, you are mine to do as I please and I say you're staying here."

She snorted, thrust her chest out and cocked her hip to the side. If he thought he could intimidate her, she had a shock in store for him.

"Well, Mr. Peter Oranye," she uttered with as much disdain as she could muster. "If you want the right to tell me what to do tonight, then you better be paying me for it. You know my fee."

Gasping, he jerked back as if she'd slapped him and his eyes narrowed.

She expected him to kick her out for her pronouncement since he seemed so averse to paying for sex. A jab of disappointment caused her chest to tighten.

She clenched her hands and shoved the feeling aside. What the fuck was wrong with her? She couldn't allow any man to control her no matter how gorgeous and irresistible he happened to be, unless he paid for the privilege. Period.

He didn't say anything for seconds that stretched into minutes. He didn't send her out of the suite either.

Feet planted apart, he crossed his arms over his chest, emphasizing the stretch of fabric across toned muscles. He glared at her, dark eyes cold and flinty.

She raised her chin and returned the glare. Her pulse pounded loudly, she swore he could hear it.

They faced each other for several thumping heartbeats, their chests heaving up and down with their panting breaths.

"Fine," he bit out. "If that's the way you want to play it."

He strode into the bedroom. Curious, she followed behind him, determined not to let him out of her sight until they'd resolved this argument of theirs.

He flicked the switch on the outside wall and entered a large closet the size of the bedroom she shared with Anuli.

She halted at the entrance and her mouth dropped open for the second time since she arrived at his suite.

On the left side, men's jackets, trousers and shirts hung neatly in an open maple wood wardrobe. Two matching tall chests of drawers and gleaming shoes suspended from racks stood to the right wall.

He pushed a rack. It made a click and slid to the side smoothly.

From where she stood, she couldn't see what lay behind the rack. His index finger moved. She heard a low popping sound before a small door opened. He reached inside. When he withdrew his hand, a wad of cash came out with it.

She gasped, amazed at another discovery. The safes she'd seen in other hotels rooms weren't hidden from view like this one which seemed built into the wall.

He shut the door, tugged the rack into place and headed back to her. Lifting her right hand, he shoved the money into her palm.

"This is ten thousand. Now, you're staying. End of story." Sidestepping her, he returned to the living room. She heard the television, a music video.

Lips pressed together in a slight grimace, she stared at the bundle of cash and fingered the crisp, clean five-hundred-naira notes. They were wrapped in a paper band with the bank logo. What did this mean? Did he now want sex? Shouldn't she rejoice because she'd won?

Instead, with slow, heavy steps, she followed his trail and stood opposite the sofa where he sat, blocking the TV from his view.

"Let me get this straight. You're paying me to stay in your hotel suite for the night. But you don't want to fuck me?"

He lowered his head onto his open hands, with his elbows to his knees.

"Peter?" she probed, wanting to understand what was going on. No man gave her money without wanting something in return. She wasn't foolish enough to believe he would do this out of the goodness of his heart. No one was that charitable.

He scrubbed his hands over his face, lifted his head and blew out a long exhale as he stared at her with eyes that seemed to look past her. "No. I'm not going to fuck you tonight."

He pushed off the sofa and walked away. She heard the bathroom door shut. Puffing out a breath, she slumped onto the sofa.

This had to be another first. A man giving her money and not wanting anything in return. Well, in Peter's case, he didn't want her having sex with any man including himself. Being paid not to have sex. It was certainly an interesting concept. Why would he do something like this? Why did he care who she was having sex with or how often? It wasn't his business what she did. Nobody else cared. Why should he?

If he'd wanted to have sex with her, then at least, she'd have understood his reasoning. But paying not to have sex was just plain weird. Was he bible-bashing evangelical trying to convert her or something?

He hadn't quoted any bible verses at her or preached at her to repent like some people did.

Her brain churned with all kinds of scenarios.

Did he not want to have sex with her? Was her job so abhorrent to him?

When she'd first met him, she could've sworn there was a connection between them, both sexual and emotional. Now she wasn't so sure anymore. There was still an emotional connection between them. She could see it in the intensity of his eyes just now. He felt something for her just as she felt something for him.

She sighed, put the money in her bag and took her shoes off. She needed the cash, if not she wouldn't be accepting it. She'd just have to find a way to truly earn it. Perhaps he'd change his mind about having sex.

She sat on the sofa and waited for him, flicking through the channels. About ten minutes later, she heard the bathroom door open. She tossed the remote on the sofa and went in search of him. She found him by the closet covered in a white towelling robe, droplets of water glistening on his head.

He'd taken a shower. He was naked under the robe.

Her skin flushed hot and her pulse rate quickened. Even dressed in something as innocent as a robe, she found him attractive.

She needed a cold shower.

He pulled a T-shirt and cycling shorts out and extended them towards her. "You can change into these so I can get the laundry team to clean and mend the rip in your dress ready for tomorrow."

"Okay." She took the clothes from him. "Is it okay if I shower?"

"Of course. Go ahead. Feel free to use whatever you need in the suite. If there's something that isn't here, just let me know and I'll arrange for it to be brought up."

He was being very cordial. There was no trace of the frustrated man from earlier.

"Thank you," she said and headed for the bathroom, grateful for the sanctuary and to be able to clean off all the sweat and partying from earlier.

"Just leave the dress on the floor outside the door," he called out.

Surprisingly, she felt a little self-conscious as she stripped in the bathroom with the door closed. She opened the door a crack and tossed the dress on the carpeted floor of the bedroom before shutting the door again. Using the hair clip in her bag, she piled her hair on top so it wouldn't get wet.

Standing under the warm shower spray was refreshing after the stressful night she'd had. She didn't get the luxury of a shower in the place she lived where she bathed with a bucket of water. So, this was pure luxury. And she savoured it for as long as she could. Even the shower gel smelled like heaven and felt lovely on her skin.

There was another fluffy towel for her when she came out. She dried herself and put on the T-shirt Peter had given her but skipped the shorts.

When she came out of the bathroom, the lights were low in the suite. Her dress wasn't on the floor anymore. Peter lay in bed, wearing a white T-shirt and covered in a sheet.

"I've had a really long day, so I need to sleep," he said. "But you are welcome to stay up, if you want to. Just keep the volume down on the TV if you want to watch."

Really? He was just going to sleep. This guy was serious about this. Okay. She could play this game.

"No. I'm tired too." She walked to the other side of the bed and climbed in. The sheets were crisp and cool against her skin as she lay on her side facing him.

He reached over and switched off the light, putting the room into darkness.

Perhaps he liked to get down and dirty in the dark. She listened to his regular breathing, expecting him to reach for her. Nothing happened.

"Peter, is there something I can do for you?" she asked, wanting to reach for him but not wanting him to kick her out of bed. She just felt weird sleeping beside a man who wasn't expecting sex.

"Go to sleep, Tessa."

She felt the mattress shift as he turned his back to her.

Feeling a pang in her chest, she sighed and closed her eyes. "Good night, Peter."

Chapter Five

She came to him like she did these days, beautiful and ethereal. At night. In his dreams. Barely there. Still full of life. Laughing. Dancing. Touching. Kissing.

"Naaza, why do you only stay for a short time?" he asked as he reached for her, wanting to hold onto her forever.

"It's because you have a life to live. I can't be in it." She smiled at him.

His throat closed and his chest tightened. This wasn't enough.

"So why do you come at all?" His voice showed his frustration at the whole situation, although in truth, he didn't know what he'd do if she didn't show up at all.

"Oh baby, it's because you're not living. You're no fun these days. You work so hard with your businesses, you don't take any time for yourself to really enjoy your life."

Her brown eyes showed her sadness, her head tilted to the side as she reached to stroke his skin. The touch whispered across his flesh. A breeze. Barely there. Still, goose bumps rose on his flesh.

"What's the point? I only wanted to enjoy my life with you. Remember the plans we made?"

"I do, honey. I also remember the fun we had. You were a man full of life, sexy and fun to have around. Now you're always so serious."

Yes, his ability to enjoy life had vanished. Fun was meeting up with his two best friends regularly and of course his family. Outside of that, he had his work, running his business. What was the point of anything else?

Naaza had been his spirit. His soul. Now, that was gone. She was gone. Only a ghost. A figment of his dreams.

It had been five years. Sometimes, it felt like fifty years. Sometimes, it felt like just five minutes. Either way, he felt as if he had no right to enjoy life without the woman he had loved for so long.

"What do you want me to do?" he asked, his voice broken by his loss.

"I want you to live, my love." She moved.

"What do you mean?" He reached for her but she slipped from him, floating away.

"Live, so I can rest…"

She faded until he couldn't see her anymore.

"Naaza," he whispered her name as he shut his eyes, tears seeping through the corners.

He lifted his hand and wiped his eyelids before lifting them to find sunlight seeping through the shut curtains of the hotel room.

He lay there, remembering his late fiancée, Naaza. She had been the one and only woman he'd loved. They'd been childhood friends who'd become lovers when they'd gone to university. They'd been inseparable and he'd even gotten his father to work it so that they'd served as Youth Corpers in the same location.

They'd made plans for the future. She was going to be a prominent Nigerian civil rights lawyer and he would be a business tycoon. One part of their plans had worked. Unfortunately, she'd died, cut down by cancer in her prime.

He'd never really gotten over her death. Never gotten involved with another woman. Many had tried to ensnare him, all to give up when he showed no interest. He'd kept out of trouble, never seeking empty release in any other person's body.

No one could ever replace Naaza.

He rolled over in bed, realised there was a woman in his bed and jerked upright. He scrambled out of bed, heart racing.

What the hell? Who was this?

He peered over the mass of hair held up with a clip to look at the face and all of last night came rushing back.

Tessa. She lay on her side facing away from him. Without all the heavy makeup, she appeared young. In her early twenties. Last night, in her gear, she had looked like she'd been in her late twenties or early thirties.

Why was a girl as young as she appeared selling her body to men?

His stomach turned and he looked away and strode into the bathroom.

Why did he have to go into that night club yesterday? He didn't know what had possessed him. He'd thought he'd have one drink and soak in the atmosphere for a short time. He'd had a hectic week and just wanted to unwind.

Instead, Tessa had knocked into him like a wrecking ball in her skin-tight dress, tower high heels and vampy makeup designed to drive a man to his knees. She'd certainly sent his mind seeking the oblivion her body would've provided. For those moments on the dance floor, he'd forgotten everything else including Naaza.

When he'd walked away from her in the car park, he hadn't expected to see her again. Yet here she was sleeping in his bed, his T-shirt skimming the curves of her body.

Arousal spiked through him, his morning wood came to life. He groaned out loud.

He couldn't do this. Why was he thinking about Tessa when the only woman he'd ever wanted was Naaza?

Guilt caused a thickness in his throat. He shouldn't have brought Tessa into his suite. He should have let her go after he'd dismissed Telema last night.

But he couldn't get the image of Telema handling Tessa, and the idea that any other man could do that to her just drove him insane. He had to keep her here.

Now what?

He stepped out of the shower and grabbed a towel, patting his wet body.

What was he going to do with Tessa now? If he let her go, she would go back to doing whatever she wanted. Tonight, she would be back at the night club, picking up more men.

His lips pressed together in a grimace and he stared down at his bare feet on the grey limestone tiles. He rubbed a hand over his chest.

What the hell was he going to do?

On the one hand, he didn't want anything to do with a call girl, a woman who sold her body for money. He was a reputable businessman. He was in Port Harcourt to discuss a potential acquisition as part of the expansion of his airline business. He should be concentrating on that. If anyone found out about his involvement with Tessa, it could scupper this deal.

On the other hand, he just couldn't shake this aversion he had of any other man touching Tessa.

If he let her go, for sure, she would be out there tonight fishing for men. She was too damned stubborn. She'd proven it by arguing with him last night and making him pay for her to stay.

He scrubbed a hand over his head, feeling the bristles of the newly cut hair from yesterday.

There was only one thing he could do.

He left the bathroom and strode to the closet, making sure not to stare at the sleeping woman. If he didn't look at her, then perhaps this constant lust he felt when she was around wouldn't overwhelm him. He'd sensed her presence last night when she'd climbed into bed. It had taken every ounce of his will not to reach for her when she'd asked if there was anything she could do for him.

Damn it. He wasn't going to be like every other man she'd met.

And he wasn't ready for another woman to replace Naaza. Didn't think he'd ever be ready even if the woman currently asleep in his bed proved irresistible.

A knock at the door had him walking across the suite to open it.

"Laundry service, sir," the bus boy said as he held out the now cleaned dress Tessa had been wearing last night.

"Thank you." He took the dress wrapped in cellophane cover, tipped the boy, shut the door and returned to place the item at the foot of the bed.

Dressed, he opened the safe and took out a bundle of cash. He walked into the living room, picked up one of the hotel notepads from the desk and scribbled a note on it. He took both the note and the cash back into the bedroom, placed the note on the bedside table next to Tessa with the cash on top of it.

He gave her sleeping form one last glance. He didn't know what her reaction would be when she saw the note or cash. But he wouldn't be here for her to argue with him as was likely to happen.

He strode out of the suite and shut the door, heading for the lift. Downstairs, he approached the receptionist.

"Good morning, Mr. Oranye," the woman greeted cheerfully.

"Morning, Rose." He made it his business to remember the names of the hotel staff he encountered. Of course, he didn't know each of the one-hundred-and-twelve employees at the Park Hotel, Port Harcourt. "Is my car ready?"

"Yes, sir. Godwin is waiting for you."

"Good. I have a guest staying in my suite for the next few hours. Please make sure she has whatever she needs."

"Of course, sir. Have a safe trip."

"Thank you."

Outside, he found the chauffeur waiting with the car door opened. He slid into the back seat as the man shut the door.

"Godwin, we need to make a quick stop over before we head to Enugu."

"Yes, sir," the man replied and drove them out of the hotel.

Chapter Six

"You know, I never thought you'd be getting married before me."

Wednesday night, Peter sat in the bar lounge at Park Hotel, Enugu with his friends. He cupped the balloon glass in his palm and swirled the clear, dark amber liquid it contained before tilting the glass to inhale the aroma. The smell of strong wood, spices and orange peel sailed through his nostrils.

He rarely drank alcohol. In fact, he could count the number of times he'd had one since Naaza passed away. Today, he needed something strong. Since he left Port Harcourt on Saturday, his mind had been unsettled.

"Point of correction. He *is* already married. This is just a formality." Michael Ede laughed at his own joke while patting Paul Arinze on the back.

"Yes, I forgot about the shotgun wedding in Lagos." Peter smirked. He truly had never thought Paul would settle down. Of the three of them, Peter had been the one who'd had a steady girlfriend throughout their university days. He'd been the first of them to get engaged. He'd thought he'd be married by now. Instead, fate had had other plans. He swallowed the brandy in a gulp.

Paul spluttered his drink, his face screwed up into a grimace. "Shotgun wedding? Ijay is not pregnant."

Peter burst into laughter, pointing a finger at him. He loved hanging out with his friends. They knew how to pull him out of his funk. "You should see your face now."

"He had you there." Michael chuckled and leaned back into his seat. He was the hot head of the group and ex-military. When they'd been teenagers, he'd always been the first to plough into a fight whenever someone threatened one of the three friends. Even now, he was their go-to man when heads needed to be bashed.

"Funny. Haha," Paul said as he dabbed himself with a napkin. Of the three of them, Paul wore his heart on his sleeves. His generosity meant that although he'd been wrongly accused and exiled by his family, he'd still welcomed them back into his life and took care of them years later.

"Are you saying you're not looking forward to babies, because you can be sure that's the next thing everyone will be expecting from both of you."

"Ha. I'm not saying that at all. There's a lot going on at the moment as it is. Ijay is relocating to Nigeria. We have all that to sort out plus the traditional wedding. Our hands are full. This is just not the right time for a baby."

"So you say," Michael chimed in. "But does Ijay think the same thing?"

Paul leaned back, his face screwed up. "We haven't discussed specifics but we're taking precautions."

"Makes sense," Peter said as his memories went to Naaza and their discussions about family.

His late fiancée had known what she wanted out of life early on. She'd been intelligent and focused but she'd also wanted to start a family soon after they'd gotten married. By now, they would've had one or two children running around their home. The dream was lost now.

"I still haven't thanked you for pulling the strings with the Attorney General," Paul said in a sober tone.

"You know it's nothing." Peter dismissed with a wave of hand. "It was the least I could do since I wasn't there myself for your wedding. Anyway, what's the point of knowing people in high places if you never use it?"

Among his friends, Peter's family was the most connected with his father's connection to politics. Chief Silas Oranye was one of the kingmakers of Nigeria politics, a member of the ruling party and a wealthy businessman.

The downside to all that was that his father held political ambitions for Peter which he just didn't want to entertain. Unfortunately, he couldn't totally dismiss it. Naaza had had political aspirations for him. She'd believed in activism and had told him that while it was important to hold the people in power responsible for their actions, it was also important to make sure that the country had great leaders. She'd seen Peter as a potential great leader.

As it was, he'd discarded any political aspirations along with her death.

"Well, your help is much appreciated." Paul fiddled with the gold wedding band on his finger.

"I hope this whole marriage thing is not contagious. First it was Michael proposing to Kasie within a few weeks of meeting her. Then you take it one step further by marrying Ijay and now we have your traditional wedding ceremony next weekend."

"You'll be next," Michael said emphatically.

"You're kidding me, right. I haven't even got a girlfriend."

"As if that matters. Look at us." Paul pointed to Michael and back to himself. "Although it took me almost six months to do anything about it, I knew Ijay was special from the moment she walked onto that balcony at the bar in London."

"Same here," Michael concurred. "When I look back, Kasie had me in her snare from the moment she walked into this bar all those months ago."

Peter stared at his friends open-mouthed. He couldn't believe how open and upfront they were being about their relationships. As a group, they didn't really discuss feelings or women in that manner. Business, yes. Sport, yes. Relationships, no way. His friends had suddenly discovered their softer sides. While he seemed to have lost his. He used to be the one all loved up and gushing about Naaza. And they would all makes jokes at him. Now things were reversed.

"I'm not sure what you guys have been taking but enough with all the touchy-feely stuff." Peter shuddered.

"Ol' boy, you're saying that now. Wait until 'the one' turns up. I'm willing to bet a huge chunk of wad that you'll be fighting to wed her in a matter of months."

"Another bet, Michael. Are you sure? Remember you lost the last one and that's how you ended up with Kasie."

"Hey, I got the girl so I'm not complaining."

"I'm backing Michael on this one, bro. I think you're going to fall hard when you meet her. I'll even go as far as to say that you'll be willing to risk everything to keep the girl. Wanna bet?"

Peter considered his friends. They seemed damned sure of themselves if the smug expressions on their faces were anything to go by. He was quite confident he wasn't getting married anytime soon. He had too many other things to deal with. His many businesses, for one.

He remembered Tessa, the defiance and desire blazing in her eyes. The way she'd clung onto him on the dance floor and made him forget everyone else.

Need curled low in his gut and his hand tightened around the glass. He closed his eyes as images of Tessa invaded his mind.

It had been this way for the past three days. He'd buried himself in work, determined to forget her. Still, when he relaxed his guard, suddenly she would be there taunting him. Daring him.

He shouldn't have invited her into his suite and allowed her to spend in the night in his bed. He wouldn't be suffering like this if he hadn't.

Now she was creeping into his mind. Slowly becoming an obsession he couldn't shake. What was he going to do? He would have to avoid going to

Port Harcourt anytime soon as he wasn't sure he could stay in the same city and not see her. Not fuck her.

"Peter, are you backing out of the bet? That'll be a first."

Peter met Paul's gaze with a smile. They thought he'd be getting married soon. If only they knew that the only woman on his mind was not a suitable wife material according to normal standards.

"You're on," he said to his friends, his lips curling in a confident smile.

This was going to be such an easy bet to win.

Chapter Seven

Tessa jerked awake, her gaze bouncing around the room in a jerky manner. A scuffing sound outside her closed door made her freeze. The house lay in darkness. Another power cut while she'd been asleep. She held her breath as she tilted her head to listen again. She heard the sound again.

Someone was coming.

Heart racing, she crept out of bed, trying to keep quiet and not attract attention. Perhaps if he didn't hear her, he would assume she wasn't here and go away.

The floor under her bare feet was cold and the chill spread up into her bones, making her wrap her arms around her nightie-clad body.

Now that she was out of bed, she wasn't sure what to do. The only means of escape was the door which separated her from the man who was surely coming for her. The other possible escape route was the window. But it had the louvered glasses, twelve in two columns. She would have to take out each individual pane to be able to climb out of the first-floor window. But that would take time not to mention that it was a noisy job. She'd tried doing it once and the hinges squeaked as she tried to slide the glass out.

Another option would be to hide. The room wasn't big. She had the option of crawling under the bed or hiding in the closet. Neither of those choices would keep her hidden for too long as he always found her.

By now, the sound outside became louder as the person thumped against the door.

Her body trembled as her pulse raced. She needed something, anything, to protect herself. Her gaze darted across the room. There was nothing in sight. Not unless one of her stuffed teddies suddenly grew sharp teeth and claws.

The door flew open and slammed against the wall. A shadowed figure stood in the space.

Her heart raced faster as she stumbled until her back hit the wall. She couldn't see the face of the person but the shape was recognisable. He was wider, taller and stronger than her.

The familiar fear returned and she muttered incomprehensibly as her breathing became choppy.

"What did I tell you about locking your door?" the voice boomed.

She cowered, hoping to make herself small and unseen. To disappear.

Chunky, fleshy hands snatched her in the dark, lifting and tossing her onto the bed.

"Please," she begged as she wiggled and kicked. But it seemed to bounce off him.

He shoved his heavy weight on top of her, holding her down and making her choke. She tried to push him away but he didn't budge.

"You know that you can't escape me. Wherever you go, I will find you."

The top of her nightie ripped and cool air rushed on to her skin just as clammy hands groped her flesh.

Her stomach roiled and bile rose in her mouth. She swallowed it down.

"*No! No! N—*"

"Tessa!"

A smack hit her across the face and her eyes flew open. A familiar concerned face leaned over her in the room lit by grey dawn light. Anuli.

She sat up, gasping for breath before she shoved her friend out of the way and ran out of the room. In the small courtyard, she bent over and threw up.

A hand rubbed her back in gentle upward strokes. She straightened up and wiped her mouth with the back of her hand.

"What's wrong?" Anuli asked.

"Just a minute." Tessa caught her breath and walked to the shared kitchen where she grabbed a cup and jug of water. She rinsed her mouth out and then went to flush the mess she'd made in the courtyard. The other tenants wouldn't be pleased to see it. Neither would the landlord.

After she cleaned up, she found Anuli in their room. They lived in a one-room studio where they shared communal kitchen and bathroom facilities with other tenants. Thankfully, the others in the building were nice so they never had any problems.

Tessa sat on the small double bed next to her friend. There wasn't much else in here aside from a wardrobe with their clothes, a desk and small chair in the corner. Next to it was their make-shift larder which had their food provisions, crockery and cutleries. They couldn't leave those in the kitchen as things tended to disappear.

Anuli sat silently waiting for her to speak. They had a good relationship and never kept any secrets from each other. Anuli knew her deepest, ugliest secrets, just as she knew her friend's.

"I had a nightmare. *The* nightmare," Tessa said, knowing her friend would understand what she spoke about. Or rather what she didn't say.

"About him?" Anuli asked as she twisted to look at Tessa, a frown on her face.

Tessa nodded, pulling her legs up bent at the knees and clasping her arms around her limbs with her back to the wall serving as the headboard.

"But you haven't had that dream in a while. A long time." Her friend was still frowning, her concern palpable.

Tessa didn't know how she could have survived these last few years without her.

"I know. It's been at least a year. I thought I was over it. And now it's back. He's back in my head." She rocked her body back and forth, her muscles tense.

"Hey, don't freak out." Anuli climbed onto the bed on her hands and knees and crawled over to Tessa, wrapping her arms around her. "You purged him from your head before. This is just a blip. Everything will be back to normal again."

"I don't know, Nuli." She used the nickname she used for her friend. "This nightmare came back because of him."

"Who?" Her friend leaned back, still caressing her arms.

"Peter. I let my guard down with him. I don't know how it happened." She shook her head. "From that first moment I stumbled into him, I let him get under my skin. I never do that with anyone."

"I know."

"So how did it happen with Peter? And what kind of man gives a prostitute sixty grand and doesn't ask for anything in return?"

She couldn't forget waking up to find Peter gone on Saturday morning. Instead, he'd left a note for her with a new bundle of cash on top of it. In the note, he'd informed her he'd travelled back to his home in Enugu. He'd thanked her for the company and wished her well.

Just like that. Her initial confusion had turned to frustration. She hadn't understood his motivations. Still didn't understand Peter. She'd had the mind to leave the money and walk away. In the end, she'd dropped the cash into her bag, showered and left the suite as soon as she could. The note had said she could order breakfast but she hadn't seen the point if Peter wasn't there to share it with her.

"He did ask for something. He asked for your time." Anuli's words drew her back into the present.

"Yes, but he paid me for it. Generously. More than anyone else ever paid me. And I actually enjoyed his company so much so that I overslept and didn't notice when he left the hotel."

"He was being super generous. I wouldn't want to leave the place too from everything you told me. I would want to keep milking him for as long as possible."

"Yeah, I know. But this seemed different. One minute he walked out on me because of my profession. The next, he was rescuing me from ending up in a police cell. How do you explain that?"

"And now your nightmare is back."

"Exactly."

"It's an omen, babe. It's a warning that no man can be trusted. You need to forget about Peter."

"I do. I can't let him into my mind. I can't go back to the nightmare again." Her voice choked, her eyes misting.

Her life had been a nightmare until she'd escaped it with Anuli's help. She'd kept men at bay emotionally, choosing instead to use sex to claim back her freedom. It had worked until Peter had turned up with his tempting smile and conservative outlook, showing her a fairy tale she could never have.

She wasn't good enough for anything else. Not without any qualifications. She was taking care of herself, earning the money for her school fees and other expenses. She didn't depend on anyone except Anuli who had been by her side through their struggles.

"It's okay," Anuli said, still caressing her body as she leaned against her.

Tessa turned her head, her lips only inches away from her friend's. "I don't want him in my head. Please, make me forget."

"Anything you want, babe."

Anuli leaned in and pressed her lips to Tessa's in a slow and gentle kiss that quickly morphed into passion as they took each other's clothes off. Soon, Anuli was kissing a fiery path down her body and was settled between her thighs, lapping at her clit.

Tessa moaned as she closed her eyes, arching her body. But as she climbed into orgasm, it wasn't the image of Anuli that she had between her legs. It was the image of Peter sliding his fingers inside her pussy as his mouth latched onto her clit.

Her eyes flew open as she came hard, her body flushed with heat.

****

Friday night, Tessa and Anuli exited the taxi outside the Xtasy nightclub. Peter had given her a nice amount of money which could easily pay for her not to work this weekend. And she'd paid the money into her savings account.

While he might live up in the clouds in his posh penthouse, she lived down in the grimy streets. In the real world, problems didn't go away. She couldn't afford the luxury of not working. If anything happened and she was ill, then she could tap into the emergency fund. But while she was still able to work, nothing would stop her. Not even the thought of Peter's disapproval of her job.

At the entrance, she slipped the burly doorman his usual fee for the night. He grabbed her arm and pulled her aside.

"Some guy has been asking questions about you," he said in a low voice.

"Who?" Anuli asked, standing the other side of the man.

"I don't know. Just some guy."

"Describe him," Tessa said, curious about who would be asking about her. Her heart rate picked up when she thought it could be Peter.

"Average height. Dark skin. Smartly dressed."

That didn't sound exactly like Peter. He would be smartly dressed but he was above average in height. And his skin was a shade lighter than hers.

"What did the guy want?"

"He wanted to know how often you came here and where you lived."

"What did you tell him?" Anuli asked.

"Well. I told him you only come at weekends—Fridays and Saturdays. But I don't know where you live so I couldn't help him there."

"Haba. How can you just be giving out information anyhow?" Anuli sounded annoyed.

"He paid me five-K. I had to tell him something. At least he doesn't know where you live."

"Good thing too," Anuli muttered and grabbed Tessa's hand as they walked into the corridor leading to the main club. The floor vibrated with the thumping base of the muted music.

"Don't worry about it," Tessa said to her friend. "It's probably just Peter asking questions about me. It sounds like something he would do."

"What's wrong with the man? Does he think you guys are dating or something? He's just a mark, for goodness' sake."

Tessa chuckled. "He does seem like a possessive boyfriend, doesn't he?" That's if it was him asking questions. "Or it could be that he wanted to know if I'll be here tonight so he could pay for my services."

The wishful idea made her heart jolt in her chest. Was Peter here tonight? Would he want to spend the night with her? Her pulse picked up speed. In honesty, she wanted to see him again.

What if he still doesn't want sex?

The thought jarred her out of the daydream. Her fingers tightened around her purse. She needed to snap out of it.

Anuli glanced over, her brows wrinkled and her gaze pained. "If he was here and he wanted you, what would you say?"

Her friend's question echoed Tessa's thoughts. Getting involved with Peter could be dangerous. Tessa couldn't afford to drop her guard. Since she'd done it once with Peter, there remained a high likelihood it could happen again with disastrous consequences next time. Anuli would have to be the one to pick up the pieces afterwards.

On the other hand, she just couldn't get Peter out of her mind. He seemed to be in her blood now. Even the sex with Anuli hadn't been able to wipe memories of him away. Usually, her friend could soothe her agitation. It had only worked temporarily this time.

She pulled Anuli into a quiet alcove that stood beside the doors leading into the main club.

"Can I really say no to the kind of money Peter flashes? Think about it. Compared to what we usually earn a weekend? Can you imagine if he turned up again and paid me to spend the night with him again? We'd be laughing all the way to the bank. Next time that you're ill or I'm ill, we won't have to worry about whether we can make the rent or whether we can buy the handouts or textbooks we need. Come on."

Anuli brushed a hand over her hair before smoothing out her skirt. "I know what you mean. We need the money. But I can't leave you alone with that man, Tess. I'm afraid of what he's going to do to you. I see the changes already happening to you and it's only going to get worse."

"So, what do you think we should do?"

"If he wants to pay for your time, then he's going to have to book both of us at the same time."

Tessa's eyes widened. Doubling up on a gig wasn't a new thing for them. Some clients wanted to have two girls so they worked together. And the fact that they were friends with benefits made it all the easier as the men loved watching them make out together.

But in those occasions, the clients usually suggested two of them. They didn't impose it on the client as Anuli was suggesting.

"Are you sure? What if he doesn't want both of us?"

"Then he can go jump. But I think he'll agree especially if he wants you as much as I think he does." Anuli grinned. "And we can double our money while we're at it too."

"One hundred grand? You think he'll pay that?"

"He's loaded, isn't he?" Anuli tugged her arm. "Come on. Let's get in there and get to work."

Tessa followed her into the dimly lit club with the strobe lights flashing over the dance floor and music pumping out of hidden speakers.

There was no point dwelling on what Anuli was suggesting. Tessa didn't think Peter would be here anyway. The description of the man by the bouncer didn't sound like him. And Peter had said that night clubs weren't his thing. He wouldn't be here two weekends in a row.

But even as she scanned the space, her heart thumped hard against her chest in anticipation. She wanted to see Peter again.

Chapter Eight

Peter sat on a black leather armchair in a darkened corner that didn't have any direct light but provided a vantage point to see most of the spacious area of the club. The place wasn't jam-packed yet. From up here in the VIP mezzanine, he overlooked the entrance.

Every time someone walked in, his heart rate kicked up a notch as his gaze flicked to the swinging door.

What was he doing here? The question had been on his mind since he arrived. He didn't have business in the city this weekend.

Still, at lunchtime, he'd informed his chauffeur to prepare for a trip down to PHC. On arrival at his suite, he'd showered, dressed and ordered dinner.

While waiting for the food, he'd fielded a call from his mother who'd asked if he could come over this weekend. He'd explained he wasn't in Enugu and would be back late on Sunday. She'd been happy to wait until next weekend to catch up with him.

After eating the meal of locally caught giant shrimps and salad, he headed out to Xtasy.

Senses heightened, his actions seemed borne of compulsion, bordering on obsession. He couldn't seem to get Tessa out of his mind. Couldn't quench the need to see her again. To finish what they'd started last weekend right here in this club.

The moment she arrived, the hairs on his neck stood erect even as his gaze riveted to the long-limbed girl who sashayed into the venue behind another smaller one. The whoosh, whoosh sound of blood in his ears drowned the music. His breath trapped in his lungs.

She'd come back here.

He became aware of the strong, rapid beat of his heart. His chest burned, acid corroding his gut.

She'd come back here in search of men. To sell her body to whomever would pay for minutes, hours or nights with her.

His fingertips dug into the smooth leather on the padded arm of the chair. Why was he bothered about what she'd come to do?

He remembered last weekend and the way they'd moved on the dance floor, everything else forgotten, the rest of the world lost to them. It had been ages since he'd connected to anyone—Naaza—in that intimate way.

The last time he'd dreamt about his late fiancée, she'd urged him to live again. To move on and have fun. The moment with Tessa last Friday had been fun. He wanted the connection again.

The urge had made him drive the almost four-hour trip from Enugu to Port Harcourt City. To see Tessa. To do more than look at her.

He wanted to touch and taste. To savour and indulge. To evoke and sate.

Still, a part of him, the sensible part that had been prominent for the past five years, warned that he shouldn't have come. Reminded him of why she was here. Her job.

Did he really want to get involved with a hooker? A woman with no emotional investment in the act of lovemaking.

Every time he'd had sex in the past, he'd poured all of himself into the act of seeking and giving pleasure, mind, body and soul. He'd never held any part of himself back.

Of course, he'd been in love with the woman with whom he'd shared those intimate moments.

Could he indulge, without giving his all, without getting emotionally entangled? He'd always been an all or nothing kind of man. In business. With family. With friends. It was partly the reason he'd never sought casual sex before.

Now staring at Tessa as she manoeuvred around the crowd of revellers, he wondered if he could keep sex between them as just fun. Of course, if he paid for her time...

Hell! He groaned and scrubbed a hand over his face.

Did he really want to go there? Pay for her services? What other option was there aside from carrying her caveman-style out of the club and locking her away in his suite?

Perhaps he should just go back to the hotel and forget this madness.

What? Leave her for other men? Hell, no! His body tensed and he gritted his teeth as anger lanced through him. He wouldn't leave this venue without her, one way or the other.

The muscles around his eyes bunched as heat flushed his face. Leaning forward, he grabbed the glass and lifted it to his lips, swallowing down the cool lemonade. He'd chosen the soft drink although most people around him drank alcoholic beverages. But he needed a clear head tonight. He needed to be in control.

Now, he couldn't be certain he'd made the right choice. If he was going to sit here and watch Tessa all night, he'd need something stronger to dull the emotions she roused within him.

The tumbler made a dull thump on the wooden surface of the table as he abandoned it and strode to the reinforced transparent glass balustrade so he could get a better view as the two girls walked over to the seating area. They found available seats and settled on them. Tessa's friend, Anuli—he assumed her to be the same one from last Friday—sashayed towards the bar.

Peter used the opportunity to observe Tessa.

Sitting, her short black dress rode up, exposing chocolate thighs and clinging to every dip and swell of her body. The black platform heels she wore made her legs stretch for miles. With dark smoky eye-shadow and deep red lipstick, the length of wavy black hair reaching her hip completed the vampy look.

She certainly knew had to dress for maximum effect. Every man in the vicinity stared at her.

Burning sensation spread across his chest and his stomach hardened as his muscles tightened.

A man in a navy slacks and pink T-shirt with D&G blazoned across the chest approached Tessa. She smiled up at him and invited him to take a seat beside her when she waved her hand to the chair. Soon, they were laughing and chatting when the other girl joined them.

After a while, Tessa and the man moved to the dance floor. They started off at a sensible distance but before long, the man pulled her close and she was swinging her hips and bumping her butt against his groin to the rhythm of the music.

Her eyes were closed and Peter wondered what she was picturing. Was she remembering the way they'd danced? A week ago, he'd been the one holding her, his crotch nestled against her cushiony bum.

His cock pulsed to life. Was he really going to stand here and watch her seduce another man in the lead up to having sex?

Before he could decide, Tessa opened her eyes and looked up in his direction.

Her eyes widened as their gazes met and he could swear she gasped with the way her luscious lips parted. She stopped moving. The man behind her leaned forward and whispered in her ear. She said something to the man but she didn't break eye contact with Peter.

Peter knew he sported an intense sullen expression but he couldn't help it. The woman drove him nuts.

She stood there, staring at him for a few seconds with bulging eyes and open mouth. Was she pleased to see him? He couldn't tell, not from her shocked expression.

Now that she'd seen him, he expected her to move away from the man holding onto her waist.

Instead, she resumed dancing while still maintaining her stare on Peter. She wound her hips, rubbing up against the pink T-shirt man who had a big grin on his face and his hands on her hips.

Fire lit in Peter's gut, filling him with possessiveness that made his hands clench around the metal pole of the balustrade.

Tessa taunted him, her intent written all over her face. The way her right eyebrow arched and her lips tilted in a lopsided smirk dared him to do his worst.

His rational mind told him to ignore her provocation. The green-eyed monster burning across his chest wouldn't hear the advice.

Hands in his trouser pockets, he strode across the floor, headed down the broad, winding staircase. He took slow, deliberate steps, keeping his gaze on Tessa, making her wait. His purpose meant to keep her unbalanced and unsure of what he would do next.

Just before he reached the bottom of the stairs, her moves faltered as if she'd stumbled and she broke eye contact.

Good. She wasn't unaffected by his presence.

Hiding his grin, he kept his face expressionless as he headed in the direction of the dance floor.

The erratic flash and dim of the strobe lighting made her fade in and out of view. But he knew exactly where she stood as he swerved around the other ravers, making a beeline for Tessa.

It seemed she'd lost sight of him as she glanced around the space, searching for him, lines appearing on her forehead. The guy behind her had his eyes closed as he rubbed up against her.

Peter stopped about a foot from Tessa. Her startled gaze fell on him.

For seconds, it seemed everyone else got dimmed and frozen out. They stared at each other separated by smoky, electrified air.

Her chest heaved as she breathed fast. Her lips parted and she swiped the bottom one with her tongue.

His breath hitched. He wanted to lick her, to dip inside her mouth and taste all she had to offer. The base of his spine tingled, his arousal spiking. He took a step, demolishing her personal space.

"Tessa, come with me." His voice sounded husky.

Her eyes narrowed and she tilted her chin up. "As you can see, I'm dancing with someone else. You can wait your turn until I'm done with him."

She pulled her lips in a saccharin smile that didn't reach her eyes.

"Hey, man," the guy behind her shouted, suddenly awakened to the situation. "Go away. She's dancing with me."

Something inside Peter snapped. A growl rumbled in his chest as his nose flared. His teeth clenched tight, making his jaw ache.

"Get your filthy hands off my girl," Peter gritted out as he leaned close to the man, injecting menace into his words. "Unless you want to get locked up for soliciting."

His breathing came fast as he balled his hands into fists. One thing attending an all-male boarding school taught him was how to brawl. Actually, he would attribute that macho skill to Michael. Still, Peter wasn't afraid of getting his knuckles bloody if necessary.

The man's eyes widened and he stepped back, letting go of Tessa. "I didn't know."

Peter used the opportunity and dragged Tessa towards the exit. He pushed through the door leading to the corridor with the bathrooms on one end and the front entrance on the other. The slab swung shut behind them, muting the noise of the club.

"What the hell is wrong with you, Peter?" Tessa glared as she tugged her hand free. "You're messing up my night."

He crowded her to the wall, caging her with his arms. "I haven't even started. How much is he paying to debase you?"

Flinching, she sucked in a sharp breath.

Okay. Low blow. But her telling him to 'wait his turn' brought out his possessive nature. If he had to drag her out of here kicking and screaming, he would. To hell with playing Mr. Nice Guy.

He didn't fucking share his woman.

His woman?

The notion had him rearing back, giving her space as he rubbed a palm over his face. What the fuck? When did that happen?

She lifted her chin again and her voice sharpened. "It's none of your business, Peter. Go to blazes. You don't own me."

"Oh, I do, Tessa." He took a step towards her. She didn't back away. "I've owned you since last Friday. Right here, in this corridor, I bought you."

She opened her mouth. "You—"

He cut her off. "But I know you. Your transactions involve cash, so I'll pay for you, your way."

She flinched as if he'd slapped her. "What? You want to pay for my time?"

"Yes." If this constituted what it took for her to stop coming to this godforsaken club as a call girl, he'd do it.

Her amber eyes flared with heat. "You can't afford me."

He ignored her insult and inhaled a steady breath. Calm settled over him. He was a businessman. Everyone and everything had a price. Including him. His price was simply different from Tessa's.

Her price was financial, a commodity he was happy to trade in.

He held her unwavering gaze. "One Million Naira."

"Chicken shit. Not even close." She turned around and headed for the door leading into the club, her shoes clicking on the hard flooring.

"Five Million," he said in a quiet voice that would carry to her. He'd expected the first offer to be rejected. This was Nigeria. Everyone haggled.

Palms flat on the door, she froze.

Gotcha! His heart thumped hard at the prospect of her accepting his bid. His hands trembled and he shoved them into his pockets. It had been a long while since he did anything this spontaneous.

After several seconds, she swivelled and faced him, frown lines on her forehead.

"Are you drunk? Did you take drugs? This isn't the Peter Oranye I met last week who walked away from me because I mentioned my job. And yet, here you are, willing to pay such a large amount of money for me. I thought you don't like call girls."

"I have nothing against call girls. I just don't use them."

"And now?"

"Now, I want you." He waved a hand at her. "And the only way it seems I can have you is to pay for you. You're selling your body and I'm buying it. A simple arrangement. This way, I make sure no one else touches you."

She angled her body away and her brow wrinkled. "Why the hell do you care about who touches me? It's my body."

"I want to be the only man who touches you!" The confession spilled out of him.

It seemed to soften her up and a slow smile curled her lips. She sashayed to him, her hips swaying with each seductive step she took.

"Well, sir. For Five Million Naira, you can touch me as much as you want," she said in a low sultry tone as she pressed her right hand on his chest just above his heart. "You have a deal."

Fuck. She'd agreed to his offer. Adrenaline rushed through him and he became breathless. Finally, he would have her to himself. In his penthouse. In his bed.

She dragged a fingertip down his chest. Even through the silk fabric of his shirt, she burned him, branded his skin. Her lips lifted in a genuine, tantalising smile, as if she'd just won a tug of war between them. He supposed it had been a battle of sorts.

"How about we get started?" She grabbed his hand and pulled him through a door.

It wasn't until they were inside and he saw the mirror on the wall and the sinks that he realised it was a restroom.

She shoved him against the wall and went down.

He grabbed her arms and tugged her up, keeping her a few inches from him. He twisted so they swapped places, Tessa with her back to the wall. "What do you think you're doing?"

She stood stock-still, staring him straight in the eyes. "I'm doing my job. You're paying a lot of money for my time, so I'm getting started."

He narrowed his eyes. "You don't have permission to touch me."

Her pulse became frantic and skittish where he gripped her wrists. She gave him that look filled with pure temptation.

"Hang on a minute. You're not going to play the same thing you did last weekend. If you're buying my time, I'm working. I presume you're not married or have a girlfriend. You're too honest to cheat." She frowned. "Unless you're gay."

His jaw tightened. "I'm not gay. I just don't believe I have to stick my dick into every woman that comes along."

She gasped at his words and glared at him. "Well, it's as well then, isn't it? Because you probably wouldn't know what to do with your dick if a woman fell on it?"

His restraint snapped and his grip on her arm tightened. "What did you say?"

Tilting her chin up, she glared at him and stood still. But she must have seen something on his face as she licked her lips. "You know exactly what I said."

This woman pushed his buttons, turned him from a level-headed man into a feral Neanderthal.

"You think I don't know how to use my cock because I haven't fucked you yet?" He leaned close, making her back flatten against the wall.

His lips grazed her ear. She shivered and moistened her lip with her tongue. "I...I..." She couldn't seem to form a word. Her throat rippled as she swallowed.

"Do you think because I've been celibate for a while that I don't know how to fuck you?" His voice came out gravelly low, just above a whisper.

"Do you think I can't make you come? That I can't make this beautiful body of yours clench and writhe and beg for me?"

She gasped and her trembling became more pronounced. "You—you're just bluffing. No man has ever made me come."

He leaned back and tilted his head. "I hear you, Tessa, and you should know I'm not a man who walks away from problems." He leaned close again and whispered against her ear, making sure to blow warm air on her skin. "So, challenge accepted."

He felt as if he was far removed from this scene and he didn't know what had possessed him. But he was still a human being and this woman made him reckless. Made him want to throw caution to the wind.

Anyway, what was so wrong in showing her? If no man had ever given her an orgasm, then he'd be the first. And then she'd shut up and stop pushing him.

He grabbed her hand and tugged her out, back into the dimly lit hallway.

"Where are we going?" she asked, keeping a step behind him.

"You'll see." He'd done some crazy things in his time. But fucking her in a restroom wouldn't be one of them. Still, he picked up on her need to exhibit and it matched his craving.

They walked back into the busy club and she followed him upstairs to the VIP lounge. The bouncer in black T-shirt and slacks who guarded the entrance let them through. Someone seemed to have taken the seat Peter had previously occupied.

Peter strode to the bar and leaned on the polished black granite counter. "You know who I am, right?"

"Sure, sir," the barman replied as he dried a glass with a tea towel. "You're my boss's friend from Park Hotel next door."

"That's right. I'm Peter and one of the owners of the hotel. I want you to do something for me."

"Sure, sir. What can I do for you?"

"Close the VIP Lounge for the next hour. I'm going to pay to use it exclusively."

"Okay. Let me speak to the manager." The man lifted the flap of the counter before walking through a side door.

"Peter, what are you doing?" Tessa asked, giving him a confused smile.

He turned to her, placed his hands on her shoulders and released a slow-building smile. "I'm being reckless and spontaneous for the first time in years. We're going to have fun."

"Fun?" She giggled. "You don't need to book the whole VIP Lounge for us to have fun."

"Wait until you find out what I have in mind, then you'll know why we need the lounge to ourselves." He winked at her.

Warmth spread through him as adrenaline spike in his blood. He would enjoy the evening and if what he suspected about Tessa proved correct, then she'd derive pleasure from their time here too.

The barman returned with the manager. Peter spoke with him briefly explaining his requirements. The manager was happy to oblige. They ushered the rest of the guests away, informing them the area was being closed for an emergency, amid murmurs of protests from those evicted.

Peter returned to the now vacant armchair in the darkened corner. He positioned the one next to it exactly the way he wanted before indicating for Tessa to sit.

"But I can't see the rest of the club from this angle." She glanced at the balustrade and back to him.

"The only person you need to look at is me. Go on." He settled in his chair.

"Okay." Her smile was back to being tempting as she obeyed. "I'm happy to stare at you all night long."

Peter chuckled. "That's exactly how I want it."

Raising his hand, he called the waiter over and ordered their best champagne.

"Well, you're in a festive mood," Tessa said after the waiter left to fulfil his request. She wore the bemused smile which indicated she still didn't understand his actions.

"We're celebrating," he replied. He'd be breaking his five-year-long celibacy.

The waiter returned with the drink along with an ice bucket. Peter indicated for him to open the bottle, which he did, pouring the sparkling light gold liquid into the flutes.

After the waiter left them alone, Peter passed one glass over to Tessa before picking up the other.

"To having fun," Peter saluted and took a sip of the bubbly drink, letting the fizz slide down his throat and loosen his limbs.

"Yes, to fun." Tessa smiled before indulging too. She drank with the proficiency of someone used to imbibing champagne.

She probably got offered the drink by clients if she came here regularly. His chest burned and he inhaled deeply to dispel the sensation. Tonight wasn't about her past or other men.

He was the man with her in this moment and he wouldn't ruin it.

Returning the flute to the low table, he reached across to place his palm on Tessa's bare thigh. The way he placed her seat meant that she sat directly facing him, her back to the aisle and balustrade. He'd dismissed the waiter and no one else was on this level with them for the next hour or so.

"So, do you still want me to give you an orgasm?" he asked as he stroked her warm, pliant skin with his thumbs. He kept his touch light, feathering her skin.

She sucked in another sharp inhale and her voice sounded breathy. "If you think you can."

"That's fighting talk, girl."

She gave him a blasé shrug. "I know what I know."

He trailed his fingertips along her sides up from her hips, keeping the caress light so that the skin was sensitised. "I'm going to make you come right here. Do you have any objections? Speak them now."

Her gaze bounced around the space before she met his and her throat rippled again. "There's nothing to say."

"Lift your dress up to your waist."

She sat there staring at him as if she couldn't believe her ears.

"Do you want to accept defeat already? If so, then you should apologise for thinking I wasn't man enough for you."

He didn't think she'd have a problem with the fact that they were in a club. After all, she'd intended to give him a blow job in the restrooms earlier. This was miles more sanitary and they wouldn't be disturbed or overlooked.

"Never," she said, her boldness returning.

His lips widened in a devilish grin. "Okay, then. Do as I say. Dress, up."

She eyed him. "Are we going to have sex in the chair?"

He undid his cufflinks and rolled up his shirt sleeves. "The objective is to give you an orgasm. How I achieve it is my business. Once you lift your dress into position, I'm in control. Are you brave enough? Or are you all talk, Tessa?"

"You bet I'm brave enough." She huffed and hiked up her dress as she lifted her bum off the seat. The hem of the dress bunched around her midriff when she sat down again.

His breath caught at the sight of all the fleshy chocolate thighs and black lace thongs.

Damn. She was sexy.

He swallowed. Heat flashed across his skin as his erection swelled. The need to feel her skin against his ramped up to another level.

She parted her legs, taunting him, giving him a view of the tiny triangle of lace covering her pussy and the string that travelled up her crack. "Now what?"

He said nothing, just kept a lopsided smile on his face as he shifted to the edge of the chair.

"Your body is beautiful and I have the mind to make you take off your dress so I can see all of you, right here." He trailed his right fingers along the side of her thigh up to where it met her left hip and knickers. "But I'll wait until we're in the suite so I can take the time to savour every part of you. It's a shame that no man took the time to show you pleasure. But I'm going to remedy that."

With his left hand, he undid the buckle of his belt before leaning back and pulling the belt out of the loops.

Her eyes widened. "What are you going to do with that?"

"I'm going to restrain you. I don't want you moving until I'm done with you. Keep your hands to your sides."

He came to stand behind her and looped the belt under her breasts, around her body, buckling it back up so that her hands were trapped at her sides and she wouldn't be able to move them.

He circled her and came around to sit in front of her.

"Is that it? Bondage? That your thing?"

"Did anyone ever tell you that you talk too much?" He hooked his fingers around her knickers. "Lift your hips."

Smirking at him, she complied and he pulled the underwear from her. Lifting his hand to his face, he sniffed it. Her musk filled his nostrils and tingles travelled down his spine to his balls.

God, he'd missed the scent of a woman. The fragrance of lust.

He scrunched the lace up in his hand, feeling the damp evidence of her arousal on his fingers.

Tessa sat bound in the leather armchair, staring at him as if mesmerised by his actions. Her pupils dilated, the pulse on her collar thumped fast. One dimmed spotlight dappled the bare skin of her parted thighs, catching the shimmer of her shaved, wet pussy.

To be this close to a woman after so many years. Adrenaline rushed through his body and his hands trembled a little. His control threatened to slip. It had been too long, almost like the first time all over again.

But this wasn't his first time. And although there seemed a lot at stake here—his reputation and his ability to redeem men in Tessa's eyes—he'd done this before. He knew a woman's body well enough. He'd learned from a Master.

He could do this. Would do this. "Open your mouth," he said as he leaned forward.

"What—"

He stuffed the thong into her open mouth. "Don't spit it out otherwise I'll gag you properly and put a blindfold on you as well."

Her eyes widened and she shook her head.

"I'll take it that you don't want a blindfold and a gag."

She nodded.

"Good." He gave a wicked smile. "Now, this is a sight to behold. You at my mercy and not mouthing off at me. One more thing to do."

He pulled the sleeves of her dress off her shoulders and undid the front clasp of her bra, making her big breasts spill out. They looked swollen and the nipples were hard and jutting up in tight peaks.

His fingers itched to touch and mould her supple flesh. To take her to the heights of pleasure again and again.

Her chest rose and fell as she took quick breaths which made her breasts jiggle.

He hardened at the sight and he imagined what it would feel like to have his cock sliding between the heavy mounds of soft flesh. His erection would be smothered as he held them snugly around him and took his pleasure.

Perhaps her pink tongue would dart out and lick his broad crown as she tasted him.

He sucked in a deep breath. The fantasy was so strong he turned into a rock in his trousers.

He reached for her, caressing her smooth skin from her knees all the way up to her thighs. Her body was soft and he squeezed the skin as his lips followed the trail his hands did.

Her breathing sped up and he could see her heart beating almost out of her chest. He nibbled and bit as he explored her body but avoided her pussy. He would make her wait to feel him there. Increase her awareness and anticipation until she couldn't bear it any longer.

His hands covered both breasts, squeezing before he lowered his head and sucked the under flesh of the right one.

"Oh...oh," she moaned, the sound muffled by the piece of underwear in her mouth. Her body arched towards his mouth, her hips canted.

"Do you like what I'm doing?" he asked as he tweaked a hard nipple between his thumb and fore finger.

"Mmhmm." She moaned again.

He continued playing with her breasts until she was writhing and whimpering, her eyes pleading.

His eyes followed the line of her body down to where her legs were spread wide. Her pussy lips were open, showing off the jewel of her clit. The opening glistened with her juices showing off her arousal.

He stroked the tip of his finger on the chocolate skin at the top of her pussy, making her body jerk. She was already so sensitive and he'd barely done anything to her. All he'd done so far was to play with her breasts.

How would she react if he nuzzled her labia, feeling the softness against his lips as he worked his way to the hard nub at the centre of her? He drew in a deep breath, taking in her scent of musk and Tessa.

Her pussy juices dripped down onto the cushion of the chair. He traced a finger around her clit. She clenched her opening, dripping. For him.

His dick pulsed. He wanted to pull it out and stroke himself. Better still, sink into her. Instead, he licked his lips as he thrust his middle finger into her slit.

She jerked her body, letting out a strangled moan. "Oh...Oh...Oh."

He slid his finger out and inserted a second one. Head back, eyes half-lidded, she arched off the chair and clenched around him. She was hot and so responsive he was at risk of coming.

"Do you know how beautiful you look?" His voice sounded husky as he shifted close to her.

"Seeing you respond to me so eagerly. I'd almost forgotten what a rush it can be."

He pumped in and out; her pussy leaked down his hand. Her body writhed as if in rhythm to the thumping base of the loud music. Her eyes widened as if she didn't expect to respond to him like this.

"Yes, I'm the one doing this to you, Tess. I found your button and I'm going to make you come."

He smiled at her as he pulled his fingers out, spreading the nectar around her clit before plunging back in, just as he took her right nipple into his mouth and suckled it. Three of his thick fingers ravaged her pussy as his thumb clamped down her on clit.

Her insides rippled around his digits a few seconds before the rest of her body jerked hard and she let out a continuous moan for seconds. She jerked again and again before going completely limp.

When he lifted his head and pulled out his hand, her eyes were closed, her breathing shallow. He reached behind and undid the belt holding her in place. She went limp in the chair, her head lolling to the side.

He wiped his hands on a napkin and looped his belt back into his trousers, his dick throbbing. He lifted the glass of champagne and drank some as a distraction from his hard on.

She opened her eyes, her expression dazed and replete.

His lips curled in a slow, satisfied smile. "So, what's your verdict? Did I redeem the men of Nigeria?"

She sat up and pulled the lace out of her mouth, squeezing it in her hand. She still wore a slightly shocked expression. "I... You more than redeemed them. Can we do that again, just to make sure it's not a fluke?"

He chuckled. "We can certainly do it again once we're in my suite."

Her eyes twinkled as she straightened her clothes, stared at the panties before stuffing them in her bag. She pulled out a flashing phone up to her ear.

"Anuli, I can't hear you properly." She held a finger to the other ear to block the sounds out.

"I'm still in Xtasy. The VIP Lounge." She lowered the phone and leaned forward. "Is it okay if my friend comes up?"

"Sure," he replied, getting to his feet.

"Yes. I'll see you in a minute." She spoke into the phone before putting it down.

Peter walked over to attendant at the VIP entrance and informed him to let Anuli in when she came up.

The girl was already walking up the stairs.

"You must be Anuli." He waved her in. "I'm Peter."

She gave him an incredulous stare before responding. "Hi, Peter."

"Tessa is over here." He led back to the sitting area.

The girl in question had moved from the chair and was not on a long sofa.

"There you are," Anuli said as she sashayed over.

"Yes," Tessa replied with a big smile on her face. "Peter and I were celebrating. You won't believe how much he offered."

Anuli glanced up at Peter before staring back at Tessa. "What?"

"Five big ones?"

Anuli pulled Tessa aside and lowered her voice but Peter could still hear them. "Do you mean fifty-K? I thought we were going for one hundred for both of us."

Peter wondered what that was about but didn't say anything as he watched them.

"No. Not Fifty G. Five Million."

"You're kidding me." Anuli glanced back at Peter and he raised his brows.

"No, I'm not," Tessa turned around with a full grin. "He said Five Million."

"Oh. My. God!" Anuli stared at him with her mouth agape. Then her face puckered in a frown as she turned to face Peter. "What exactly do you want from us?"

"Us? I'm paying for Tessa. Not both of you." His back stiffened. What was going on?

"That's where you're wrong, sir. You see, we come as a package deal." Anuli placed her arm around Tessa's shoulders. "If you buy one, you get the other."

"Tessa, what's going on?" He didn't like the way Anuli was smirking at him as if she knew something he didn't.

"Well, Mr. I'll-buy-you. You just got yourself a bargain. You bought one—" she pointed at her chest and then at Anuli's, "and you got a second one for free. Are you man enough for two women or are just chicken?" She cocked her brow.

Shit. He'd just been had. Outmanoeuvred. Played by a player.

If he said yes, then he'd have to take both. But if he said no, then she'd walk back into the club and he'd be back to square one.

Chapter Nine

"Now that you have us up here, how do you want us?" Tessa asked, sashaying across the living space of the suite and perching on the corner of one of the sofas.

Anuli followed her, her walk slower as she glanced around the room with a bright smile on her face as if she admired the space.

Peter shut the door to the suite with a click and stood there as he sucked in a deep breath. The situation had run away from him in the night club. He'd underestimated Tessa.

He'd had no option but to invite both girls up to his suite. He certainly hadn't wanted to rehash the negotiations of buying Tessa. Neither had he been willing to let her walk away from him.

Thankfully, he was one of the owners of the hotel and although the night receptionist had glanced over at him and the women as they'd waited to catch the lift, the man hadn't said anything. He dreaded to imagine what the rumour would be once he passed on the information to the rest of the staff.

Peter couldn't worry about that. He had his hands full with what he would do with these two women now they were in his suite. The time in the lift had made him think a little bit more clearly and he now had a plan of action.

"How about two of you just relax? Would you like something to eat or drink?" Peter said as he waved at the room, projecting charm and nonchalance. He didn't exactly feel carefree but he couldn't show the women anything else.

When he'd headed down from Enugu to Port Harcourt earlier on today, he hadn't known the day would end with him buying not just one but two call girls. This was so out of character for him, his friends and family might call an intervention if they found out.

"Sure," Anuli said. "I'm actually hungry."

Peter strode across to the desk and picked up the room service menu. In this kind of situation, it was important to focus on the practicalities. Get the adversary to relax. Food and drinks were a good way to start. "Order whatever you want."

Anuli took the booklet off him with a smile that looked genuine. He was still learning her so he wasn't totally sure.

"Thanks. I will," she said.

He glanced at Tessa who seemed to be watching him with a curious expression. "Don't you want something to eat, Tessa?"

"Yeah, I'll have something. I'll take a look when she's done. I'd like some champagne too. Can we have champagne?"

Something about the gentle way she asked seemed to be a contrast to the brash girl from the night club. Sometimes, it was as if he couldn't

117

recognise her. As if she was two different people. Certainly, the woman he saw today seemed different from the one he'd met last week. He couldn't pinpoint why.

"Sure. Of course. I'll order a bottle or two with the food," he replied.

"Thanks." Tessa stood up and walked across to where Anuli sat down. "What are you getting?"

Peter left the girls and went into the bedroom. There was something he needed to do to wrest the situation back into his control. He pulled out his phone and dialled the number for his lawyer.

"Okey," he said when the man answered. "Sorry to disturb you late on a Friday night."

"It's not a problem. I was working anyway," the man replied. "What can I do for you?"

"I need you to draw up a contract for me. It's urgent and I need it tonight."

"Tonight?"

"I'm afraid so." He didn't usually demand this type of work from his lawyer. But the man was on a retainer and knew the demands of Peter's business. Peter could call on him at any hour of the day.

Okey sighed. "What do you need?"

Peter listed the items he needed on the agreement before the man hung up saying he would get back to him within the hour.

He ended the call and made another one to the hotel manager.

"Christopher, I'm going to need you to come up to my suite later tonight sometime in the next thirty minutes to one hour. I'll let you know when."

"Sure, sir. Just let me know when you're ready."

Peter tucked his phone back in his pocket and returned to the living room.

Tessa, who'd been lounging back on the sofa, sat upright when he walked in. She appeared wary, her eyes narrowed as she bit her lip. In contrast, her friend Anuli seemed not to have a care in the world. Her chin was high and she had a gleam in her eyes.

It was easy to see the contrast between the two women and their similarities. They wore similar clothing and makeup and they did the same job.

But somehow, it seemed Tessa was the more fragile one. She deferred to Anuli's judgment. At least, that's what he'd noticed since he'd been in both their company. It made him yearn for the Tessa he had met last week. That one had fire in her eyes and had challenged him. This one still challenged him but it felt as if Anuli was the one pulling the strings, which bothered him. He wanted to separate them and see what Tessa would do.

"Have you decided what you're having?" He sat at the desk which provided distance from the girls and picked up the hotel phone.

"Yes." Tessa sashayed across with the menu in hand and pointed out the food they wanted.

He indicated to the chair next to his and gave her a charming smile. "Sit down."

Her eyes widened at she met his gaze. She glanced behind her to where Anuli seemed engrossed in a movie on the large TV screen. She met his gaze again and he nodded encouragingly as if she were an injured animal that he had to get to trust him.

She lowered her body onto the chair and he placed his hand on the exposed skin of her lower thigh. Her breath hitched and he could see the fast-beating pulse at the base of her neck.

Her skin was warm and velvety. He stroked the edge with his thumb as he told the guy on the end of the phone what he wanted to order.

Tessa's leg trembled and she tried to pull away. He tightened his grip, not letting her go and not glancing in her direction as he carried on talking to room service. When he finished his call, he replaced the handset on the cradle before turning his full attention to Tessa.

"Do you remember last weekend?" he asked in a low voice so that Anuli wouldn't overhear above the sound of the television.

She held his gaze as if unable to look away and tugged her lower lip between her teeth before nodding.

He settled his left hand onto her right thigh while the other hand stroked her left thigh.

"Do you know that I thought about you all week?"

"You did?" Her voice was low and breathless. It was as if they were having a conspiratorial conversation.

He leaned forward, still maintaining eye contact. He watched as her eyes turned into the amazing liquid gold.

"Yes, I did." He sucked in a gulp of air. "I couldn't wait to see you again, which is why I came to PHC this weekend. I came here for you."

Blood whooshed in his ears as he licked his lips.

"And finding you at Xtasy, having you bound on the chair in the VIP Lounge while people partied downstairs. You were fucking beautiful. Your intoxicating scent, the feel of your pussy as it clamped around my fingers, the way your body arched and trembled much like it's doing down. I will never forget it."

She was trembling like a leaf in the wind, her breathing shallow and coming quickly.

He pushed the seam of her dress up her thighs. As if she couldn't help herself, she lifted her hips so he could shove the dress above her hips and out of the way. She wore nothing underneath as her discarded thong was in her purse.

"Would you like me to make you come again?" he asked, keeping his voice low as he leaned in to nuzzle the side of her neck.

She tilted her head to the side, giving him room. He scraped his day-old bristle against the sensitive skin there.

He leaned back to look at her face. "Would you?"

She licked her lip, swallowed and nodded as if she was afraid to speak.

"Say it, Tessa. Tell me what you want me to do to you." He needed her to concede to him, even in this small way. He wanted it to come from her. Not because Anuli was egging her on or telling her what to do.

Her throat rippled as she swallowed again before speaking. "I want you to make me come, Peter."

"Good girl." Warmth spread across his chest. He smiled his approval as he placed a kiss on her shoulder. He brushed his fingertips over her hip, feeling the warm skin underneath.

She spread her legs, moving them to the outside of the chair, so that he had free access to the moist flesh between her thighs.

Using his left hand, he stroked over her right breast while his right fingers slid over her slippery silky skin.

"Unnnnh," she moaned long and low.

The sound pleased him to no end and spiked his arousal, making his heart pound in his chest as heat flooded his skin. He wanted her to make that sound again and again, so he continued stroking the labia and around her clitoris in a circular motion.

She rocked her hips in rhythm as his fingers pumped past her opening into her soaking wet pussy. Her eyes fluttered shut and she let out a long exhale as well as a restrained, almost silent sob.

His cock turned to rock in his trousers and he stifled a groan. It seemed he needed this as much as she did. Maybe more. Not having been with a woman for so long, perhaps he needed to prove to himself that he could still perform. That his encounter with Tessa earlier hadn't been a fluke.

Her eyelids fluttered shut as he slid a second finger into her, hooked them inside her and ground his palm against her clit.

She rocked her hips in a slow circular motion, fucking his palm. Her grip on the arms of the chair tightened and she tilted her head to the back of the chair. Her pussy pulsed around his fingers. From the last time, he knew that her orgasm wasn't far away.

He leaned forward and latched his lips on the junction of her neck and her shoulders, tracing his tongue along the line and tasting the salt on her skin.

"When is the food coming?"

The sound of Anuli's voice made him freeze. He felt the tension on Tessa's body too as she stiffened.

He lifted his head and met Tessa's widened gaze that read of embarrassment and shock. He tilted his head to the side, curious about why she would be embarrassed about his hand in her pussy on the verge of making her come while her friend was asking questions about food. She looked as if she'd been caught doing something she shouldn't.

Well, he'd bought her. So, this was now his game to dictate. Neither she nor Anuli could say otherwise.

He glanced in Anuli's direction. The sofa she sat on had the back towards them so she had to twist to see them. In between them were the dining table with six chairs. Coupled with the fact that Tessa's chair backed her, Anuli had no direct view of what they were doing.

"Food will be here soon," he said in a loud voice for the benefit of Anuli.

"Good. I'm so hungry," Anuli said before turning to face the TV. "Tessa, come and check out this movie."

Tessa stiffened and tried to get up.

He shook his head and didn't take his hand out of her. "Tessa will be there soon."

Tessa's brows scrunched up as she gave him an enquiring look as if she wondered why he wasn't letting her go.

He probably should let her go back to her friend. But that would be giving in to Anuli and once tonight had been enough.

He shook his head, emphasising his refusal by clamping down on her clit. She gasped; her eyes fluttered shut before flying open.

"Please," she whispered in a breathy voice.

There was such vulnerability in her pleading voice, which made his hand still. At the same time, a knock sounded on the door, making her stiffen again.

"Anuli, open the door," he said.

"Sure." She got off the sofa and headed for the door which was on the other end of the suite.

With a final flick of his thumb on her clit, making her mewl, he withdrew his fingers. He raised his glistening digits up to her lips. He didn't need to tell her before she opened her mouth. Her tongue darted out and swiped his hand, tasting her juice and licking it clean.

"We're going to finish this later." He pulled out his handkerchief and wiped his hands as he stood up.

The door had been opened and two busboys strode in with the trays of food. They placed the food on the dining table. Peter tipped them before they left. He turned around to find the girls already at the table, opening the dishes.

He watched them and the enthusiastic way they tucked into the meal, eating and chatting about the movie on TV.

Occasionally, Tessa would glance his way and meet his gaze. It was as if she couldn't look away from him. Then she would be distracted again by something Anuli was saying.

His phone buzzed and he excused himself to take the call. It was from his lawyer to confirm that he'd sent the email with the contract. Peter thanked him, hung up and called Christopher.

"I'm sending a contract to the printer in your office. There'll be three copies. Please bring them up to my suite," he said to the man.

"Sure. I'll be up shortly."

Peter ended the call and opened the app for his email. He found the one he needed and downloaded the file. Then he sent it to the printer in Christopher's office to be printed.

Ten minutes later, there was a knock at the door and he strode across to open it. His manager stood at the door and Peter waved him in. "Come in."

The girls looked up as he and Christopher stood beside them.

"This is Christopher, the hotel manager," Peter introduced as he took the sheaf of papers from the man. "This is a contract I need you to sign to confirm our agreement."

Tessa's cutlery clattered onto the table as her mouth dropped open. Same as Anuli.

Anuli seemed to recover quicker. "A contract? You want us to sign a contract with you?"

"Of course." Peter returned the smirk she'd been sporting when she'd mentioned package deal back in the night club. "You didn't think I'd just hand over five million to you ladies without any legal paperwork to back up the sale."

"I...I..." Anuli stuttered as she raised her hand to her mouth.

Tessa shook her head as she gave him an incredulous stare. "I didn't see that coming."

She sounded as if she couldn't believe he'd done this. Well, they weren't the only ones who could pull surprises out of the bag. This should even the odds between them.

Chapter Ten

Tessa's hands shook and the fork clattered against the white bone-China plate, the sound echoing in the silent room.

Peter wanted them to sign contracts. This didn't bode well at all. Why had Anuli convinced her to do this deal with Peter? Why had she agreed to it?

Simple answer: Money.

Peter had been so generous last week. She'd thought perhaps she could earn some easy cash. But by the looks of things, he wasn't going to make things easy for her or her friend.

Peter tossed the file of papers on the table and shoved his hands into his pockets. He stood between Anuli and Tessa, so close that if she shifted in her seat, she would brush against him. His posture was strong, legs planted apart, chest thrust out.

She had to tilt her head back to look up at his face. He met her gaze. The determination in his gaze made heat prickle over her skin and she looked away. He unsettled her. Intimidated her. What had she gotten herself into?

Still waters run deep. Peter was a conundrum.

Letting out a sigh, she got off the chair at the dining table and walked over to the sofas, choosing one as far away from Peter as possible within the suite.

Anuli stayed at the table, reading the contract. Tessa didn't even want to read it, didn't want anything to do with it.

This was another side to Peter she hadn't expected. He'd been so good to her last weekend, she'd almost forgotten the hardnosed determined man who'd seen off Telema and rescued her. How could she have forgotten that when she'd challenged him, he'd risen to the challenge and given her a mind-blowing orgasm, something no other man had done before?

He was a man with resolve and accomplished whatever he set his mind to. Tonight, his resolve was focused on her. It didn't matter if Anuli came with the package. He was determined to get what he wanted. Tessa.

She could see it in the way he stared at her even now she sat far from him.

That look sent a sizzle of anticipation down her spine and heat of desire pooled low in her belly. Her pussy clenched as she remembered the slide of Peter's thumb over her clit.

Suppressing a moan, she tossed her head against the back of the sofa and closed her eyes. Was she willing to throw away her freedom for the five million naira—two point five, since half was Anuli's—and the promise of another orgasm?

She could get orgasms from Anuli. Her friend knew her body well enough.

Tessa opened her eyes and turned in the direction of the dining area but didn't look at Peter who was still standing silently along with the hotel manager.

"Anuli, let's get out of here," she said as she pushed off the sofa and grabbed her bag.

Anuli's head jerked up and she gave an incredulous stare. "Why?"

Tessa's skin prickled. She knew Peter was looking at her but she still refused to look at him. "I don't want to sign the contract."

Anuli shoved back the chair, wood scrapping on carpet. She walked across the room with the contract in hand. "But you haven't even read it. I don't see anything bad in it."

"What do we know, Anuli? We're not lawyers. I bet he got his lawyer to write it up. We should get a lawyer to read it before we sign it."

Anuli pulled Tessa's arm, dragged her to the corner and lowered her voice. "We can't afford a lawyer, remember? And I'm not about to dash a huge chunk of money we're getting on this deal to some lawyer just for him to tell us it's okay to sign the contract."

"But Nuli, this was supposed to be just some easy weekend gig. Now signing a contract makes it more. It's as if he's buying us. He's going to own us."

Anuli frowned before glancing away and flapping her hands. Tessa understood it meant her friend was agitated with the situation. Same as Tessa.

Her friend swallowed before speaking. "I know he'll own us. But it's only for a period."

Something in her friend's voice made her stiffen. This wasn't going to be good. "A period? How long?"

Anuli lifted the papers, turned the page and pointed to paragraph. "One year."

"One year!" Tessa's voice rose as she swivelled to find Peter sitting on one of the dining chairs, along with the manager. He seemed busy on his phone but looked up at her.

"You're keeping us for a year?" she asked, unable to hide her shock.

His left brow quirked up. "You didn't think I'd pay five million just for a weekend. I'm no money-miss-road," he said with disdain and returned to his phone as if unaffected by her shock.

What the hell? Her mouth dropped open and closed again. What had she gotten herself into? She wasn't about to stay here and play this out. She'd never win at this game that Peter was playing and she had too much at stake. Too much to lose.

Turning to Anuli, she shook her head. "We have to go."

She turned to walk away but Anuli held her arm. "Tessa, calm down. Listen to me."

"What?"

"I've done the calculations. Say we're earning fifty grand every week for the next year, which you know only happens around festivities or when a big roller comes into town which is like once or twice a year. But say we're earning fifty gees every weekend for one year. That's two point six million each. This guy is giving us two point five million each. Guaranteed. This is the best deal we've ever had, babe. Think about all our plans."

Tessa's anger fizzled out and she sighed. "I know, Nuli. But we choose different men for a reason. We don't want to give any man control."

"I know. But you said he's a good guy, right? And we're going to be together all the time. And you know if he tries to hurt anyone of us, I won't let him. You know that, right?"

Tessa nodded her head as she swallowed a lump in her throat. Her friend had gone to great lengths in the past to protect her, even putting her life in danger. But she wasn't sure Anuli could protect her from Peter. Somehow, she sensed the threat from Peter wasn't going to be physical but at a level that neither Anuli nor anyone else could help her.

Tessa would have to work doubly hard to protect herself any way she could. She couldn't let Anuli down. This money would be life-changing for them. Anuli needed the money as much as she did. Her friend had always done so much for her. A year would soon fly by. And as long as she had her friend with her, then she'd hopefully survive whatever Peter threw at them.

"Okay. Let's do it," she said to Anuli.

Anuli pulled her into a hug and whispered in her ear, "I won't let him hurt you."

Tessa didn't miss the threat in the other girl's voice. She also knew Anuli meant it. She squeezed Anuli around the midriff. "I know."

Anuli released her and stepped back. "I'll let you handle him. We know he likes you so let's use it to our advantage. Come on."

They walked to the dining table and settled in the seats they'd been eating in. She sat at the head of the table and she used the position to boost her confidence. Anuli wanted her to take control of the situation and she would as far as she could.

They pushed the plates aside.

"We're ready to sign the contract," Tessa said as she gave Peter a determined look.

Peter leaned back in his chair, one arm on the tabletop, his body angled to the side to face Tessa and the other hand on the back of the chair separating them. Peter's pose proved he was the figure of authority in their little gathering.

The next year was going to be full of power tussles to find out who was in charge.

"This is a simple employment contract that has been amended to accommodate our special arrangement," Peter said in a steady voice. "But if you want to get a lawyer to look it over before you sign it, I'm happy to wait until tomorrow for you to sign it."

And prolong the situation further? No. He was being reasonable but she wasn't willing to wait. The sooner they got started, the sooner the year would be over and she could have her life back. Plus, Anuli was right. Lawyers were expensive. They couldn't afford one.

"No. That's not necessary. Just give me a moment to read through it," she said as she turned to the first page of the contract.

"Sure," he said but she didn't look up.

The document appeared like a normal contract, not that she'd seen many of them in her life. But she'd signed a tenancy agreement for the place they lived so she'd seen legal documents before.

She read Peter's first name and surname as well as his address which was listed as this hotel. There were black spaces in the first paragraph for her and Anuli to add their names as the named 'Employees.' She spent time thinking of the words which were written in plain English mostly. There wasn't a job title although there was a clause that stated that the 'employees were to perform the duties as specified by the employer.'

"It doesn't specify the actual job," she said as she glanced at Peter.

"Well, we all know you're here as my escort. But I'd rather not have that written in black and white. My requirements are not complex."

"But how do I know you won't ask us to do something unreasonable?"

He met her gaze and said in a calm voice. "What do you classify as unreasonable?"

She couldn't think of anything so she glanced at Anuli who gave her a shrug. "I don't know. Anyway, we don't work during the weekdays."

He gave a slow grin that annoyed her. How did he manage to be so unruffled?

"I saw you at the club on Friday night."

She huffed. "Yes. We work Friday nights but not from Sunday night to Friday night."

"For five Million Naira, you'll work any day I say," he said with a touch of arrogance.

"Then the deal is off."

"What?" The grin disappeared from his face.

She struggled not to smile at the little victory although her stomach churned. She didn't really want to walk away from five million but some things were non-negotiable.

"We only work certain days. You either take it or leave it." She hoped she wasn't screwing things up and glanced at Anuli who nodded at her in approval. She breathed in relief that at least her friend supported her in this.

Peter's eyes narrowed, his brows wrinkled in a frown as his gaze darted between Tessa and Anuli. "Are you seriously telling me that you don't work during the week?"

"That's what I'm saying." She leaned back into her seat and eyed him.

"Why don't you work during the week? What do you girls do?" He shot glances at them.

Tessa sucked in a deep breath and said in as calm a voice as she could muster. "Every employee is entitled to time off work. What we do in that time is private and none of your business."

He shoved his chair back and stood up, pacing away and back. His body was tense, his shoulders muscles coiled and his hands clenched.

Tessa's hands trembled on the table. Had she pushed him too far and blown it? Was he angry with her? Was he going to back out?

The warmth of Anuli's hands covered hers and she turned to her friend who smiled reassuringly. Anuli's trust in her made her really want to get this deal so that they didn't have to worry about money any longer. But there was a line neither of them was willing to cross.

From the corner of her eye, she saw Peter swivel and stride back to the table. She turned to face him as he stood beside the chair he'd been sitting on.

"You know once you sign this contract, neither of you are allowed to be with any other man for the next year," he said in a tight voice.

"Hang on a minute," Anuli cut in before Tessa could reply. "Are you saying we can't have boyfriends or date?"

Anuli had a smirk on her face which Tessa understood the meaning. They didn't have boyfriends and had no intentions to get any. But the question was valid. Employers couldn't tell employees when to date or not to date.

"We all know neither of you date—" He did air quotes with his index fingers, sarcasm dripped from his voice. "—so, let's cut the crap. In clause fourteen, it specifies that you're not allowed to have any sexual contact with other men during this period whether you're giving or receiving it and whether you're being paid or not."

Shit. What? She'd read clause fourteen but thought it only meant she wouldn't work with other men. She read it again and now it became clear. He really was being specific. She couldn't have sex with another man for the next year aside from him. Knowing him, that was probably not going to happen, no matter how many times he gave her ecstasy.

She didn't care about not having a boyfriend but should she really be agreeing to this on principle? Could employers do this?

"As an employer, you can't tell your employees when to date or have sex. This is oppressive and against our human rights." She was reaching but what the heck? Why not?

"Yes, I can. The law allows it when there's a conflict of interest. When you do certain jobs on a full-time basis, the contract of employment specifies that you can't do a similar job for another firm. Some firms won't even let you to work for them if your spouse works for a rival firm."

He sat back on the chair, his upper body leaning forward with his arms on his thighs.

"The work you're going to do for me involves using your body. I'm paying you to work for me exclusively. I can't permit you to then do the same job for another person whether they are paying you or not. So, if you want the five million, this is going to be an exclusive deal."

Tessa swallowed hard. What he said made sense. This wasn't a conventional job so different rules applied. Still, this wasn't a deal breaker so there was no point getting hung up on it.

"So, if we agree to exclusivity, do you agree to let us have Monday to Friday off?" If he agreed to this, there was no reason this shouldn't work out for all of them.

He held her gaze for a few racing heartbeats where she thought he'd changed his mind. In the end, he nodded and smiled. "Yes. You'll be free from Sunday night until Friday night, although I'd like some flexibility as to the exact times."

Her chest lightened as a huge smile broke out on her face. She glanced at Anuli who was smiling too. "Of course, we can be flexible about times."

If they could get to classes on time on Monday, there wouldn't be any problems.

"Good," he said as his eyes twinkled. He really did look handsome when he smiled.

Her cheeks heated up as he caught her gawping at him. She focused on filling out her name and address on the document before signing it and handing it over to Anuli who did the same.

She had a bit of unease about giving out her full name and home address. The only other place with that information was the school registration. But Peter knew nothing about her past so it shouldn't be a problem. So, she shoved the feeling aside.

Once Anuli signed the copies, Peter did the same and Christopher signed as witness. Peter gave each of the women a copy while he held onto one.

"I think we should celebrate," Peter said as he picked up the bottle of champagne and popped the top.

Anuli cheered and Tessa smiled as butterflies fluttered in her belly. When she met Peter last weekend, he woke something inside her and she knew he would have an impact on her life. She could only hope that it would all be positive and the next year would be full of cheers.

Chapter Eleven

Peter stood hyperaware of everyone in the suite as he took a sip of champagne. The bubbly liquid fizzed down his throat into his belly even as the satisfaction he usually felt at the completion of a successful deal spread warmth across his chest.

He'd bought businesses and secured contracts worth billions of dollars in his lifetime. He'd built firms from scratch and seen them grow under his leadership.

Yet, this wasn't like any deal he'd ever done before. He'd never bought another human being before.

Okay, technically, he'd bought Tessa's time last weekend. Still, that had being just for the night. Their time together had mostly been innocent, if you ignored the fact that he'd craved her while she lay in bed with him. Of course, he'd finally given into temptation and had caressed her body to climax tonight.

Now he'd bought two women. Had them at his disposal for the next year. Fifty-two weeks. Three hundred and sixty-five days.

"Sir, I'm going to head down now." Christopher cut into his thoughts as he placed his empty glass on the table.

He gulped down the rest of his bubbly and disposed of his glass. "Thank you for all your help. I'll talk to you tomorrow."

"Sure. Good night, sir. Bye, ladies." He headed for the door.

"Bye, Christopher," both girls chorused as they giggled.

Peter followed the man and placed the 'Do Not Disturb' sign outside the door handle. He didn't want to be interrupted for the rest of the night. Not that anyone came up here unless summoned.

He locked the door. From here, he heard Tessa's laughter at something Anuli said. The throaty sound sent tingles down his spine. Heat spread across his groin as a smile curled his lips.

That had to be one of the most beautiful sounds he'd ever heard. He couldn't remember her laughter being this carefree when she'd spent time with him last Friday. He had to admit that Tessa and Anuli shared something more than just ordinary friendship.

The ease with which the other girl eased Tessa worries about the contract had amazed him. It was obvious Tessa trusted Anuli more than she trusted anyone else. More than she trusted him.

His ribs squeezed tight at the thought. He couldn't possibly be envious of the relationship and trust Tessa had for Anuli. They'd obviously been friends a long time. He'd only known Tessa for a week. She couldn't trust him as much as she trusted her friend.

Yet, he was envious. He wanted her to be as relaxed with him. To laugh at his jokes with the same abandon.

Well, there was no point skulking around the corner listening to them talk. If he wanted to gain Tessa's trust, then he had to be front and centre in her life. He had to become her focus.

He'd have to find a way to get rid of Anuli. In the meantime, nothing would stop him from having fun.

The word 'fun' reminded him of Naaza. He closed his eyes briefly and silently prayed his late fiancée approved of his choice of fun. She'd been sexually adventurous.

Although they'd both been each other's first lovers, they hadn't wanted to stumble upon things. So, they'd researched and read books and had even visited sex clubs together while they'd been on holiday to the USA. Naaza hadn't been a shy girl. She'd known what she'd wanted out of life, sex and her man. And Peter had made sure he'd acquired as much knowledge as possible so he could give her everything she wanted.

Now he strode back to the dining table. Tessa glanced at him. Her eyes sparkled with humour, her body relaxed in the chair.

He smiled at her as he picked up the second bottle of champagne and popped it open. Then he picked up his glass, holding both it and the bottle in his left hand as he took Tessa's arm with his right hand. He'd been craving physical contact with her all evening and couldn't keep his hands off her any longer.

"Come," he said in a low voice. "Both of you."

Tessa stood slowly. She swayed and he caught her.

"Are you tipsy?" he asked.

"A little." She giggled. "The champagne went straight to my head."

"Light weight," he teased as he hooked his arm around her shoulders to steady her and guided her to the sofa.

Anuli brought the glasses and placed them on the coffee table. Peter waited for her to sit before guiding Tessa to the opposite sofa. Placing the bottle on the table, he sat down and pulled Tessa down between his spread thighs.

As soon as her bum hit the leather couch, he tugged her so her back was against his chest. She tensed for a few seconds as if reluctant to relax onto him. But he increased the pressure until she sighed and leaned against him. Having her softness against his body felt good even as her scent filled his nostrils.

"Anuli, get a bottle of water from the fridge and bring a glass." He kept his voice soft even though he was giving an order.

Anuli frowned but she still obeyed and got off the sofa to do his bidding.

Divide and conquer had been a technique used for millennia and he wasn't averse to using the same strategy if he needed it.

With Anuli gone, he leaned forward, brushed hair away from Tessa's face and asked, "How are you feeling?"

She moaned and turned her head to look up at him, a seductive smile curling her lips. "I'm fine. Just a little horny."

She rolled her hips, bumping her ass against his crotch. Arousal spiked through him, turning his cock to granite. He groaned and his grip on her hair tightened.

He needed a woman's wet heat wrapped around him. Better still, he wanted this woman's pussy clenching around him.

"That's good, Tessa, because I plan to make you horny and give you plenty of pleasure over the next year." He stroked her skin as her breath hitched.

She frowned as she looked up at him, her expression filled with curiosity and awe. "You're paying me—us—to give you pleasure. Yet, you're so focused on giving me pleasure. Why is that? I don't understand you sometimes."

She sounded genuinely miffed. He spent a few seconds studying her face. Her insecurities sat just below the amber gaze. Something clenched at his heart and fury rose at those who had hurt her in the past and turned her into the woman she'd become. This woman that didn't trust men enough to choose one above all others.

He brushed his lips over the frown lines on her forehead. "First of all, I'm not paying you to give me pleasure. I'm paying you to do my bidding. They are different things."

He leaned back to meet her gaze. "Secondly, it's obvious to me that some if not all of the past men in your life have either caused you pain or have been negligent in showing you the joys of ultimate sexual pleasure. I want to let you know that I'm not those men. I'll gratify you in all the ways it is possible for a man to satisfy a woman in the matters of the flesh."

Anuli returned with the bottle of water. She poured some into a glass.

Peter didn't let go of his hand in Tessa's hair and extended his left hand to Anuli.

"It's okay. I'll give the drink to Tessa." Anuli walked around the table.

But Peter kept his hand outstretched. "Give it to me."

The frown on Anuli's face deepened. "Why?"

He cocked his brow. "Do I really need to explain? You are here to do as I say. I want Tessa to drink from me. So, pass me the glass and sit down."

He really wasn't in the mood to argue with her tonight. He'd paid the first instalment of five hundred thousand naira each into their personal accounts via online banking tonight. The next instalment was due in three months, assuming neither of the girls backed out before then. They'd accepted his money. It was time to play ball.

Anuli seemed taken aback by his no nonsense tone and handed him the glass. He waited for her to sit down thinking she would disobey. She didn't and lowered herself onto the leather couch with a huff.

He lifted the cool glass to Tessa's lips. "Drink."

She did so obediently. At least, he didn't have too much to worry about with Tessa. She could be meek sometimes. The problem was with Anuli.

When she emptied the tumbler, he leaned across and returned it to the table. He returned his left hand to Tessa's thigh, caressing it lightly with his thumb.

"I was saying to Tessa that for the next three hundred and sixty-five days, the two of you are my responsibility. I take my responsibilities seriously. As such, I work with rules. You keep to my rules, you get rewarded. You disobey them, you get punished."

Tessa stiffened in his arms and turned her head. "Punished?"

"Yes," he replied emphatically.

"What kind of punishment?" Anuli asked.

"It can be whatever I think is suitable for the offence. But I promise you it is best to avoid them."

"So, what are the rules?" she asked.

"The first one is about health. As was stated in the contract, you'll both undergo physical screening and tests. Tomorrow morning, I'm taking both of you to the clinic so we can all get tested for HIV and other STDs. It'll give each one of us peace of mind. Next week, I'll arrange for you to be examined by a doctor to make sure there are no other health matters that need investigation."

Tessa nodded and Anuli didn't say anything although she avoided looking at him. "What else?"

"The next thing is your appearances. While I understand that you needed to dress the way you did to attract attention, this isn't necessary anymore. You have my attention. So, from now on, you both need to tone down how you dress. I prefer the understated classy look."

"Does that mean we're going on a shopping spree?" Tessa asked with amusement.

"Yes, after the visit to the clinic, I think you girls will need the retail therapy." He stroked Tessa's hair.

"That's great. I have no problem with that," Anuli said.

"Good. The other thing is the hair. You'll need to get rid of the weaves and wigs. I want you girls to be as natural as possible. And that includes the fake nails too."

"What? No." Tessa twisted, her eyes widened.

"Yes." He gripped her nape, holding her still. "I don't want you hiding behind all the hair and nail extensions, all the loud make-up and clothes. I want to see the real you, Tessa. Same goes for you, Anuli."

Tessa shoved at him and he let her go. She stood up and hurried across the suite into the bedroom. He heard the door to the bathroom slam shut.

He looked over at Anuli. She glared daggers at him.

"What the fuck are you doing?" Anuli said, her voice raised as she stood, hands akimbo. "Why would you tell her you want to see the real her? What are you going to do when you see the real her? Do you even know what you're asking for?"

Peter's gaze on Anuli didn't waver and he didn't lose his temper at her raised voice or rude tone. He'd been expecting this kind of response from her at some point. It was interesting to witness it so early. Even more interesting that Tessa had gotten upset because he'd wanted to find out about the real her.

"Anuli, I know what I'm asking and I think it's only fair. What you see of me is the real me. I don't hide anything about myself. So, I see no reason for either of you to hide behind masks. We're going to be spending a lot of time together. The better we know each other, the easier it will be on all of us."

She opened her mouth as if to dispute and closed it. She closed her eyes, tipped her head back and puffed out air before lifting her eyelids.

"Listen, I understand what you're saying. But you need to let go of this thing you're planning. Tessa is never going to trust you. She's never going to be the kind of woman you think you want. This is not *Pretty Woman*. This is the real world. There isn't going to be a happy ever after for the two of you. Don't pretend like there's going to be. I won't let you mess her up."

It suddenly hit Peter then. This protectiveness Anuli had for Tessa. It wasn't just the protectiveness of a friend or sister. It was more. It was possessiveness, as if Tessa belonged to her. He recognised it because it was the same way he felt about Tessa.

This led him to one conclusion.

"You and Tessa. You're not just friends. You're lovers. You're in love with her." His body chilled as he spoke the words and they settled like heavy weights on his shoulders.

She didn't say anything for several seconds that seemed like minutes. But her gaze didn't waver and her expression was rigid. Eventually, she said, "Yes. We're lovers. But it's not what you think. Yes, I love her and I will protect her with my blood. Even if it means shedding someone else's blood."

In his life, no one had ever issued a threat directly to him to his face. But Peter knew a threat when he heard one. Anuli was being loud and clear.

His response was two-fold. Utter admiration for this woman who would stand up to him, and intense jealousy for the relationship the two of them shared.

He understood the protectiveness. He'd felt it a long time ago for another woman. And yet, he knew he felt it on another level for Tessa.

Despite Anuli's threat, he wasn't put off. He was even more determined. He stood up. He wasn't about to have anyone railroad him from his plans.

"You and Tessa are adults and you know very well this deal is just an arrangement. I haven't made any promises that I don't intend to keep. So back off."

He turned to walk to the bathroom but swivelled to face Anuli. "And another thing. You don't have permission to make love to Tessa again. If you touch her without my permission, be prepared to face the consequences. I promise you won't like them."

"You wouldn't dare." She eyeballed him.

"Well, dare me and find out, if you're brave enough."

He didn't wait for her response and headed to the bathroom to find Tessa.

Chapter Twelve

Tessa sat on the cover of the WC bowl, her head on her hands, elbows to knees. The back of her throat hurt and tears built up at the behind her eyeballs. She had to squeeze her eyes tight so as not to spill them.

What had she gotten herself into? What was wrong with her?

She should be angry with Peter for making the demands he was doing. And yet, a part of her couldn't build up any anger at him.

She'd stormed out of the living room and taken refuge in the bathroom purely because she'd been afraid.

Afraid of what he was asking of her. Afraid of what he would find out about her. Afraid that if she allowed him to get a peek into her real life that he'd be disgusted with what he found out about her.

She didn't know why she had this irrational fear but she did. He'd been the one man she'd met in almost forever who'd treated her with any kind of dignity. Who didn't just want to use her?

And she was afraid of ruining it. Afraid that his reactions to her would change if he found out who she truly was.

It was best he knew her as she was. Tessa, the call girl.

Life would go on as normal. Him having no expectations or her and her having no expectations of him.

But it seemed that line may have already been crossed. Because Peter had expectations and so did she.

She liked—enjoyed—the way he treated her. She wanted to bask in his presence, to soak up his aura, to writhe beneath his touch.

What was she going to do?

Now that she was here, she didn't want to walk away. Not just because she'd accepted his money and would have to pay it back. But because she genuinely wanted to be here with Peter. And Anuli, of course.

A knock on the bathroom door made her stiffen. She lifted her head. Perhaps Anuli had come to find out if she was okay.

She cleared her throat and asked, "Who is it?"

"It's Peter. I'd like to come in. Is that okay?" His gentle deep voice sounded muffled through the door.

A small smile curled her lips. This was the thing she couldn't understand about this man. Sometimes, he came across as hardnosed. And yet, at other times, he showed such consideration.

After all, he now owned her. This was his suite. He didn't need her permission to go wherever he wanted in this space. Yet he was asking her. The door wasn't even locked.

How could she hide herself from him physically or emotionally? He was tearing down her walls with very little effort.

She stood up and walked to the mirror, taking a wad of tissue to clean up her face.

"Yes, you can come in."

The door handle twisted and the slab swung inward. Peter stepped in and closed the door behind him.

Her stomach flipped over and her heart thumped hard in her chest. She kept her head straight, staring into the mirror. Still, she couldn't resist peeking at him with the corners of her eyes as she continued dabbing under them.

He stepped close, standing behind, close enough for her to feel his body heat but with no physical contact. He stared at her reflection, meeting her gaze.

Her hands trembled and she closed her eyes, afraid he would see how much she wanted his proximity. How much she wanted him to hold her right now.

Where did that come from? She'd never wanted this kind of contact with a man. Yet, she yearned for him so much, she physically ached right now.

"I upset you. I didn't mean to."

Her eyes flew open and she gawped at him.

"You're apologising?" When had any man ever done that for her?

"Yes." He swept the hair off her shoulder and settled his cool hand on her nape, sending shivers down her spine. "I don't want to hurt you, Countess. That's not what this is about."

Hang on. Did he just call her countess? As in a member of nobility. Her? No. She must have heard him wrong. He must have said Tess and she misheard him. Her imagination was certainly running away with her.

"This whole set up is meant to be fun for everyone," he continued, speaking as he caressed the skin of her neck making it sensitive. She barely suppressed a whimper. "But I'm afraid I'm not very good at light and flirty. I don't do things by halves. It's all in or all out for me."

"Don't I just know that?" She laughed. He was the most intense guy she'd ever met. From the moment she'd met him, he'd been profound, passionate and powerful. She couldn't even imagine him any other way.

He smiled, his face lighting up and making warmth spread through her. She liked seeing him smile.

"I hope you'll bear with me. I'm not trying to make life difficult for you or Anuli. I just can't get involved with people I don't know very well. It's the same thing with me in my business dealings. It's the reason I own businesses with my best friends. I trust them with my life so I know I can trust them with my investments. Do you understand, Tessa?"

See, he didn't call her countess. She mentally shook her head.

"Yes, Peter. I think I understand. You want to get to know me and Anuli better. It makes sense. And anyway, since we won't be working—" she chose her words carefully, "—with other people for the next year, it makes sense not to wear our work clothes or look like pros. I get it."

"Good." Smiling, he tugged her shoulder so she had to turn around to face him.

Her heart thudded hard. It was one thing to stare at him in the mirror. Now that she was facing him and he stood so close, the lust was even more pronounced.

She swallowed the hard lump in her throat. "Can I ask for something, please?"

He tilted his head to the side, his hands on her shoulders as if he didn't want to let her go. "Sure."

"I will answer questions about me and my life here in Port Harcourt. But please don't ask me about my life before I came to live in this city. That life is dead and buried. I don't talk about it. I don't want to resurrect it."

He stared at her for moments on end. She thought he would reject her request because it was taking him such a long time to respond.

"Tessa, believe me, I understand about painful pasts," he said finally, making her puff out the breath she was holding. "I understand wanting to bottle it all in, to block out the pain and not think about it. Believe me, I understand."

A shadow passed over his eyes and he looked tormented. She recognised that look. Something bad had happened to him too. Her heart clenched for him. She didn't know when she reached across and pulled his body to hers, wrapping her arms around him to offer him comfort silently.

"So, if you don't want to talk about whatever it was that happened, I won't insist. But you should know that you can tell me anything in confidence. I won't judge or criticise." He pressed his lips to her forehead and held her tight.

She wanted to believe that he wouldn't judge her. That he wouldn't take offense to what had happened in her past. But she couldn't trust him like that. He was still a human and humans were fallible. She couldn't bear to see disgust or disapproval on his face when he found out.

No, it was best like this. The past would stay hidden as far as she was concerned.

She sucked in a deep breath taking in his scent into her lungs—musk and man. So arousing and so comforting at the same time. She could get used to this. She didn't believe that she had a whole year of this man in her life.

A man who seemed to care about her at least on some level.

"Will you do something for me?" he asked in a low voice that drew her out of her musings and focused her attention back on him.

She leaned back and looked up at his face. His expression was still intense and her breath caught as her skin flushed. "Okay. What is it?"

"I'd like to wash your body in the bath. I want to clean away the scents and tastes and touches of other people on your body. It's symbolic more than anything else. I want to make you pure for me. Will you let me do that?"

"Okay...yes." She didn't know what else to say. She was too flabbergasted. Too speechless. He was asking to bathe her. He didn't have to ask. He could command and she'd do it. It was what she'd signed up for. But him asking made her choke up. And him wanting to wash away her pasts made tears build up behind her eyeballs again.

She lowered her gaze. He couldn't physically wash away her past. But she appreciated that he wanted to do so mentally. Psychologically.

"Good." He pressed his lips on her forehead again before turning around. "You can get undressed while I run the bath."

Watching him lean over the bath, she curled the long tress of hair into a tight bun at the top of her head and held it in place with a head band. Peter plugged the hole. She took her dangling earrings off and placed them on the counter. He reached for the bottle of bath cream by the side of the bath before he turned the faucet on. The sound of running water filled the space as she pulled the hem of her black dress up and over her head.

With dress in hand, she looked up to find Peter staring at her with open desire in his eyes. She had doubted that he was attracted to her since they hadn't had intercourse last Friday.

There was no doubt in the way he looked at her now. He wanted to devour her.

It made her surprisingly nervous. Her hands shook as she clutched the dress to her midriff. Why was she nervous? She got naked in front of men all the time.

Truth was, she wanted Peter's approval. Wanted him to want her. To not dismiss her. To give into the lust between them. *Please.* Wetness dripped down her thigh from wanting him. If he didn't do something, she would go nuts.

"Give me the dress. I'll get it to the laundry service while you're in the bath."

"Okay." She swallowed and handed it over, bringing her hands back to her midriff.

"Go on. Take the rest off. Unless you want to go in with those stilettos." His grin was boyish and mischievous.

She smiled in return. "No way. I'm not ruining perfectly good shoes. They cost me a fortune."

Reaching down, she tugged off the high heels before unhooking her bra, setting her heavy breasts free. Her nipples stood erect showing off her arousal.

He let out a low whistle as his gaze roamed her body, heating her flesh in a trail. "You're beautiful, Tessa." His voice was thick and guttural. "Get into the bath before I forget my resolve and fuck you here and now."

He stood up and headed for the door. When the door shut behind him, she let out a sigh as she stepped into the warm water covered in bubbles and smelling of coconuts. She lowered her body and leaned back at the end of the curved bath. She let out another sigh as her body relaxed to the warmth and scent and feel of water on her skin. She'd never had a bath like this. This was another first courtesy of Peter.

She heard the door open. She lifted her eyelids and saw him re-enter the bathroom. He had rolled his sleeves up past the elbows. Her heart was back to thumping hard as her breath quickened.

Smiling, he walked over and sat at the edge of the tub. "How are you feeling?"

"Great. I've never had this kind of bath before. It's relaxing. I feel as if I could fall asleep in here."

"I'm glad I was able to give you this first too. But don't fall asleep yet." He picked up a sponge and started rubbing it against her skin, using the bubbles and water. He started with her shoulders and worked his way down to her chest, over and around her breasts down to her stomach. Then he rubbed her left thigh and lower leg down to her toes and back up the right leg to her hip. He reached up and washed her face gently.

"Lean forward," he said.

She did and he washed her back down to her bum. Her skin tingled, getting sensitive.

He tossed the sponge. "I don't need it for this part."

She leaned back as he dipped his hand into the water again down to her groin. She closed her eyes as his fingers rubbed over her labia and down over her opening. His touch wasn't sexual, almost functional, although her body still responded to him.

"Tessa, look at me." His voice rumbled.

She met his gaze, as captivating as always.

"Promise me that from today onwards, you won't give your body to anyone else but me. Promise me that whatever your need, be it sexual or financial or whatever that you'll come to me first to resolve it. I don't care about what you've done in the past or who you've been with but from today onward for the next twelve months, promise you belong to me only."

It was as if he held his breath waiting for her answer. Her heart clenched tight. He was giving her that all-consuming look, as if he couldn't look away from her. As if in this very moment, his whole life was focused on her.

She felt powerful. Important. Perhaps for the first time in her life.

Peter wasn't ashamed to admit how much he wanted her. Almost needed her to make this promise. To become his.

And she wanted to be his. "Yes, I promise."

He blew out breath. "Thank you, Countess. And I promise to take care of you in every way I can for the next year."

That word again. She reared back. "Did you call me Countess?"

He gave her the most charming smile she'd ever seen on his face. "Yes, I did."

"Why? I'm not a countess. I don't have any royal blood. As you know, I'm a call girl."

"No. Not to me. The call girl is dead as of tonight. You are now my countess."

Her eyes watered. What was this man doing to her? This had to be some dream. It couldn't be happening to her. It wasn't reality. "You're not for real, Peter."

"I am, Countess. Last week, you said something that touched me deeply. You said you could never be with one man, never give one man everything. Well, I want to show you that there are decent men out there. Hopefully by the end of our time together, you'll learn to trust men again. And when the right man comes along and gives you his heart, you'll accept it and give him yours too."

Her heart ached. Their time together would be temporary. He was preparing her for another man. He wasn't going to be the man after this year. Were there other men like him? She doubted it very much. She hadn't met them before.

"I don't think such a man exists. Well, aside from you." Her throat was scratchy.

"Trust me, there are many good men. But for now, I want to be the good man in your life. Let me show you how good this life can be."

He leaned forward and captured her mouth. *Oh. My. God.* He was kissing her. Peter was actually kissing her. For the first time since they'd met. His hand gripped her nape, holding her still while his mouth devoured her, his tongue invading her mouth, stroking, caressing.

Her body bowed off the bath, wanting more contact with him. She reached up and grabbed his shoulder, getting his shirt wet in the process.

He didn't seem to mind and didn't pull away. Instead, his right hand covered her heavy left breast. He squeezed; she moaned. He tweaked the nipples between his thumb and index finger; she writhed. His right hand slid down past her belly button to the junction of her thighs. She spread them apart without much thought wanting him inside her like she'd never wanted anyone.

His fingers stroked her folds down to her clenching entrance. Fingers plunged into her just as he broke the kiss. She was panting for air as her body tightened and heat rushed over her skin. He kept pumping his digits into her, brushing her clit with his thumb.

"You are so beautiful. So fucking beautiful." His voice was rough as he bent over and took her nipple in his mouth.

She moaned again, losing herself to the sensation running amok in her mind and body. Ripples spread out from her core and she knew she was close.

"Show me your pleasure, Countess. Come for me." He flicked her clit with his thumb and thrust inside her.

She detonated, thrashing around and sending water splashing everywhere including over the bath and on Peter as she cried out again and again. "Oh...oh...oh!"

She didn't know how long her orgasm went on for. She only opened her eyes when Peter lifted her out of the water and slowly slid her onto the bathmat. Her knees trembled and she clung on to him so that she didn't fall.

He reached across, grabbed a towel and slowly patted her down. He gave her another towel to wrap around her dried body.

"Go on into the bedroom. I'll be out shortly."

She stared down at the bulge tenting his trousers and her cheeks heated up. "Are we going to have sex tonight?"

"I thought we just had sex." He gave her that boyish grin again.

Her cheeks heated again. "I... I know. I meant are you going to fuck me with your dick? It can't be right that you're always going without."

She rubbed the balls of her feet on the bathmat, feeling ridiculously out of sorts.

His hand cupped her chin and he tilted her head up so she would look in his eyes.

"You don't have to doubt that I want you. The evidence is clear as day. But I haven't been inside a woman for a long time and I want it to be right between us for the first time."

"You mean it's going to happen?" A slow smile spread on her face.

"Yes, it's going to happen. I want to bury myself so deep inside you. I ache from wanting you so much. Trust me. It's going to happen, just not tonight."

He captured her lips again in a fierce kiss that left her panting when he broke it.

"Go on," he said, his eyes twinkling. "Get out of here before I change my mind and fuck your brains out."

"Promises, promises." She teased, feeling confident about her place in his life for the time they would be spending together.

He swatted her bum. "Cheek."

She yelped and giggled as she sashayed out of the bathroom. For the first time in months, perhaps years, excitement raced through her. She was looking forward to spending more time with the same man. With Peter.

Chapter Thirteen

Tessa practically bounced on her feet as she walked into the bedroom. A song that had been playing in the nightclub came into her mind and she hummed it as she walked over to the closet.

Last week, Peter had allowed her to wear his T-shirt. She assumed he wouldn't mind if she helped herself to another T-shirt tonight. She opened a drawer, found folded briefs, shut the drawer and opened another. Neatly folded T-shirts sat in a row. She picked the first white one and shut the drawer.

Pulling the T-shirt over her head, she let it slide down her body and let the towel drop to the floor. The soft cotton felt good against her skin. Knowing this was Peter's filled her heart with joy. It was as if wearing his clothes made her feel closer to the man.

She picked up the towel and tossed it in the wicker laundry basket she found in the closet. She sauntered out of the closet, still humming and halted in the bedroom when she saw Anuli standing by the door to the living room. The song died in her throat.

Her friend stood feet planted apart, chest thrust out, elbows wide and hands on hips. Her nostrils flared and her eyes were cold.

Tessa easily recognised Anuli's anger but she didn't understand it. Especially since she was practically floating with happiness. Had something happened while she'd been in the bathroom?

"Anuli, what's wrong?" She took steps to her friend, concern making her cross the large space quickly.

"You're asking me? What did the two of you do in the bathroom?" Anuli lifted her chin up and her eyes narrowed as if in suspicion.

Tessa's cheek heated up at the accusation in her friend's voice. "He ran a bath for me and he washed me. He said he wanted to clean me and make me pure for him. We both know how ridiculous that sounds, right?"

She laughed nervously and stopped when Anuli showed no sign of amusement. In fact, her friend's expression seemed to harden.

"Did he touch you? Did he give you an orgasm?"

Tessa pulled her bottom lip between her teeth and licked it. Her friend was making her feel embarrassed about what Peter had done to her and it made her want to deny it. But she had never lied to Anuli and she wouldn't start now. She would rather not say anything.

She angled her body to walk past her friend who was occupying a chunk of the doorway with her hands akimbo.

Anuli grabbed her hand, stopping her. "Tell me the damned truth. Did he make you come?"

"Jeez, Anuli. What is wrong with you? Yes, he touched me. Yes, he made me come." She snatched her arm away and stomped into the living room, all her happiness now fizzling away.

She grabbed the remote control from the low table and dumped her body on the sofa. One advantage of staying in this hotel was that she didn't have to worry about power cuts and she could watch as much TV as she wanted. They didn't have a TV in the room they shared. But one of their neighbours did and sometimes, they went over there to watch some shows or movies.

The channel playing on the big screen was showing music videos. She flicked through trying to find an African movies channel.

Anuli stood in front of the TV, blocking the screen.

Tessa sighed and stared up at her friend who still looked angry. "Anuli, why are you so angry? What have I done wrong?"

"I'm angry because you're letting him split us up." She came around and sat on the edge of the coffee table in front of Tessa.

Tessa muted the TV and dropped the remote. "Him who? You mean Peter? He's not trying to split us up."

"What do you think he's doing when he takes you into the bathroom so the two of you can be alone and he starts touching you?"

"But I was the one who went to the bathroom because I was upset."

"And I had an argument with him and told him off for upsetting you."

"You did?" Was that why Peter had come into the bathroom to apologise? She'd been surprised when he had.

"Yes, I did. You know I can't stand to see anyone upset you." Anuli placed her hands on Tessa's bare knees.

"I know. Thank you." Tessa covered Anuli's hands with hers as she leaned forward. "But you don't have to worry about Peter. He won't split us up. We're best friends forever."

"But, Babe, I worry." Anuli lifted Tessa's hands and clasped them together with her hands on the outside. "I worry that he'll seduce you with his money and his words. I worry that you'll believe his bullshit and that in the end he'll hurt you. Because we both know that no man is good. This is all an illusion."

"Nuli, you worry too much. Anyway, I think Peter is a good man—"

"You see?" Anuli reared back. "You already believe his words. He's already convincing you. He gives you two orgasms and you think he's Saint Peter."

Tessa frowned as her cheeks heated again. "It's not like that."

"Isn't it? I used to be the only one who could make you come. Now the two of you sneak off to be together and you ignore me. I'm part of this deal also, or have you forgotten?"

Shifting in her seat, Tessa averted her gaze. When her friend put it like that, she did feel as if she was sneaking around with Peter.

"I knew he was touching you earlier in the dining room when you guys thought I couldn't see you. I know the sounds you make when you're aroused, Tessa. I know how you sound when you're close to an orgasm. I'm not stupid, you know?"

Tessa swallowed, feeling even more embarrassed and guilty. "I know you're not. But I can't help it. When he touches me, I melt."

"You also melt when I touch you, don't you?" Anuli lowered her hands to Tessa's thighs, pushing them apart. She cupped Tessa's bare pussy with her right hand.

Tessa sucked in a sharp breath, her heart racing. Her pussy was sensitive after her recent climax and Anuli's fingers roused her again.

But there was something not quite right about having her friend touch her intimately this time. She couldn't put her finger on it.

"Anuli, don't." Tessa gripped her friend's hand and tugged but Anuli didn't budge.

"Don't? Am I suddenly not good enough for you anymore?" Anuli raised her voice.

"Shh. Lower you voice. It's not that. You're my best friend. I just don't want Peter to know about us." She tried to appease her friend and hoped she would see sense.

Anuli already thought Peter was trying to split them up. That would never happen. She didn't know what Peter would do if he found out that she and Anuli were lovers. He could call off the deal and make them return the money he'd paid.

Anuli's expression hardened again as she glanced behind Tessa and withdrew her hand from her pussy.

"He already knows." Anuli pushed off the sofa and walked away toward the bedroom.

Tessa turned around and found Peter standing by the bedroom door as Anuli shoved past him.

He didn't respond to Anuli's aggression. Instead, he was staring at Tessa with an unreadable expression.

She scrambled off the sofa and stood rigidly, her hands clasped together in front of her.

Oh Lord. Had he heard their conversation? Had he seen what Anuli was doing to her? How could she live this down? What was he going to do?

He didn't do or say anything for moments that stretched like hours. Her body trembled.

Was he going to kick her out? What should she do?

"Peter, I... I can explain," she said finally, unable to stand the silence any longer.

"I'm listening." His voice was cold. It was the only sign that he'd seen or heard something he wasn't happy about.

Her heart shrank. She'd upset him. How was this evening going from bad to worse? First it had been Anuli's anger. Now it was Peter's she had to deal with.

Sucking in a deep breath and puffing it out, she narrated what had happened when she'd come out of the bathroom, seeing Anuli angry and trying to reassure her friend that Peter didn't have an ulterior motive.

"She was upset that you weren't including her in the interactions. And she has a point. This deal includes her."

"Only because you girls insisted. But how I execute it is totally at my discretion. I'm paying her two point five million naira. She shouldn't be complaining."

He had a point. He could decide whatever each of them did. "But—"

"No buts, Tessa. Your friend knew the deal she signed up for. I call the shots around here. She can either accept it or get out."

He sounded so harsh. Tessa swallowed. "I know. I'm sorry."

His chest heaved and some of the tension left his body. "So, were you really not going to tell me that you and Anuli were lovers?"

She averted her gaze and shook her head, feeling worse.

"So, you were going to lie to me? At least your friend had the decency to confess it when I confronted her about it."

She sucked in a sharp breath and covered her open mouth with her hand. Anuli told him?

He walked past her, picked up the remote and switched off the television.

"I can put up with the fact that you sold your body for money. I can put up with the fact that there are things in your past that you don't want to tell me. I can even put up with the fact that it is highly likely that you will cheat on me. But what I will not put up with is a person who tells lies. So, in the morning, you can take your things and leave. I don't want to see you again."

He was sending her away. Her heart shrivelled, her stomach sank.

She rushed to his side, fell to her knees and clutched the grey, silk PJ bottoms he wore. "Please don't send me away. I promise I won't ever lie to you again. Please."

He sighed and tugged her arms, pulling her to her feet. "I'm serious, Tessa. I can't stand liars. If I find out you lied to me again, I'll kick you out without hesitation."

"I know. I'm sorry. It won't happen again," she said, hoping for a reprieve.

"Okay. You're forgiven." He placed a kiss to her forehead.

"Thank you." Her muscles were weak with relief and her body trembled. She'd thought it had been over between them.

He took her hand. "Come on. Let's go to bed."

She followed him as he switched off the light in the living room.

In the bedroom, she stared at the huge bed. At least, it was massive enough to fit all three of them.

But there was a problem as both she and Peter were covered in clothes. Anuli wouldn't have anything to wear aside from the dress she wore tonight. Her friend had been right. She didn't want her to be excluded.

"Is it okay if I pick a T-shirt for Anuli to wear to bed?" she asked.

Peter turned as he strode to the side of the bed. "Yes, sure. If you get her dress, I'll drop it off for the laundry service."

"Thank you." He was back to being generous and she was grateful.

She walked into the closet, picked a T-shirt and strode across to the bathroom and knocked.

"Come in," Anuli said.

Tessa walked in and found her friend in the shower cubicle.

"I brought a T-shirt for you to wear so your dress can be cleaned tonight," Tessa said.

"Okay. Thank you," Anuli replied.

Tessa placed the T-shirt on the counter and picked up her friend's discarded clothes. Outside the bathroom, Peter waited with a laundry bag. She put the dress and underwear in it.

A couple of minutes later, a knock came at the door.

"Get into bed. I'll drop this off." He took the bag and headed back into the living room, the light coming on.

She hesitated for a moment, wondering which side of the bed to sleep in. At home, she slept on the left and Anuli on the right. But this was Peter's bed and Anuli was going to join them. In the end, she crawled onto the bed and placed herself in the middle.

Peter came back just as Anuli came out of the bathroom. He strode over to the side of the bed closest to him—the left, while Anuli climbed into the right side.

Neither of them spoke as they settled on either side of her. The bed was big enough that they didn't touch.

Tense, she lay on her back, staring up at the white ceiling waiting for someone to say something.

Eventually, Peter rolled over and kissed her on the forehead. "Goodnight, Tessa. Anuli."

"Good night, Peter. Good night, Nuli," she said.

"Good night," her friend mumbled and turned over on her side.

Peter switched off the lights, turning the room into darkness.

Tessa closed her eyes. It occurred to her she was lying between two of her lovers. She needed each of them in different ways. Her bond with Anuli was psychological. They were bonded by their pasts and the things they'd done since.

Yet, she had a bond with Peter too. It was physical but so strong and powerful, she couldn't think of letting it go. At least not yet. Not for another year.

She had to find a way of appeasing each of them so that she didn't lose her best friend or the man that she seemed to be getting attached to.

How she was going to do that, she didn't know. The thoughts whirled in her head until she fell asleep.

Chapter Fourteen

Tessa was pleased that both Peter and Anuli seemed to have sheathed their swords and called a truce the next morning.

Breakfast was uneventful. They sat down together and ate the meal of sausages, scrambled eggs and toast while Peter outlined the plan for the day.

While she wasn't too thrilled about the trip to the sexual health clinic, she understood the necessity for all their sakes.

After eating, they showered, got dressed and headed downstairs.

Peter told her to head on to the car while he spoke to the receptionist.

Outside, a chauffeured car waited for them. It a Mercedes Benz GL63 SUV and the man introduced himself as Godwin.

"Good morning, Aunty Tessa," the man greeted her as he held the back door open. He was somewhere in his 30s from what she could tell and was dressed smartly in short-sleeved white shirt and navy trousers.

She smiled. "Morning, oga Godwin. How now?"

She spoke to the man in Pidgin English hoping to keep a casual tone between them.

"I thank God o," he asked.

"This na my friend, Anuli." She introduced her friend as she got into the car.

The man nodded at Anuli with a smile. "Welcome."

"Thank you," Anuli said as she joined her in the back seat.

She didn't have to know about cars to know how expensive it was. The immaculate interior, the fresh smell and the softness of the cream leather as she sank into it told the story.

Peter came out of the entrance. Instead of sliding in beside Anuli, he shut that door. He spoke to the chauffeur but she couldn't hear what she said to him. He walked around to the other side of the car and opened the door where Tessa sat and slid in.

She shifted so she ended up in the middle seat. The car had three rows of seats but it was interesting that they all chose to sit on the same row.

After that, they headed for the clinic. Each of them saw the consultant privately before the tests were conducted. Then they sat in the reception and waited about thirty minutes. The waiting had to be the longest. Peter's phone rang and he stepped outside to take a call.

Anuli reached for her when they were alone. "You know whatever the result, you're still my babe."

Tessa puffed out a breath and smiled. She was glad that she still had her best friend. "Thank you."

They were called back in individually and given the results of the test. Thankfully, her results came back negative. So did Peter's and Anuli.

Afterwards, they grabbed a quick lunch to go before they went shopping for new clothes. There wasn't time to fit in hair appointments but they managed to book one for the next Friday.

They were exhausted by the time they got back to the hotel. That night, they chatted easily while eating dinner. None of the arguments from the previous evening came to the fore.

Sunday went too quickly for her. They had brunch after which Peter headed back to Enugu. This time, she had his contact details and he had hers.

The week went too slowly for her. Interestingly, Peter called her every evening. Because Anuli was usually in the room with her, she tried not to stay on the phone with him as long as she would've liked. The more excited she became about talking to and seeing Peter again, the more withdrawn Anuli became.

On Friday, Tessa left school early to head to her hair appointment. She'd booked it so it would be done before she saw Peter. She wanted him to see her without the hair extensions. Anuli's hair appointment was on a different day but she agreed to accompany Tessa to her appointment.

Afterwards, they headed over to the hotel. They'd left some of their things over there as Peter had said they could come there whenever they wanted. The suite was reserved for him permanently.

She'd been surprised that Anuli had come along with her. Because of the way her friend had been behaving all week, she'd thought she'd refuse to meet with Peter. But Anuli had come along too.

About seven o'clock, her phone buzzed. She grabbed her phone. It was Peter.

"Hey," she said as soon as she picked up the phone. Her excitement filtered through her voice.

"Hey, Countess," he replied. "How are you doing?"

A huge smile broke on her face like it always did when he called her countess. "I'm great. We're waiting in the hotel suite. How about you? Have you arrived?"

"I'm sorry, Countess. I'm still in Abuja. My meetings ran late. I've only just finished and heading to the airport. I'm going to be late getting to Port Harcourt."

Her shoulders fell. "Oh. Are you still coming tonight? Isn't it late?"

"Don't worry about it. I own an airline, remember? I'll be in PHC in a few hours so don't stress. Just relax. Order whatever you want and I'll see you soon."

"Alright. See you soon and be safe."

"I will. Be good, Countess," he said and hung up. He always signed off that way.

Her shoulders slumped as she stared at her phone.

"What's the matter?" Anuli came to sit beside her.

"Peter is still in Abuja," she said and leaned back on the sofa.

175

"Ha. Abuja? That means he's not getting here until tomorrow because it's too late to catch a flight."

"That's what I thought but he said he would be here in a few hours."

"Tomorrow morning is still a few hours. He was just telling you that so you don't worry. So, what do we do? Go back home?"

"No. He said we should stay and relax. We can order whatever we want."

"Good. Because I wasn't planning on going back home anytime soon. Have you forgotten there's been a power cut for days? Who wants to miss out air conditioner and DSTV?"

Tessa laughed. They were enjoying luxuries in Peter's suite compared to where they lived. "You're right."

Anuli turned on the TV and Tessa hunted for the room service menu. They hadn't eaten since this morning before they headed off to classes. They ordered food along with a bottle of wine.

They sat on the sofa, eating the food, drinking wine, and chatting about the general gist in school or the movie they'd been watching. The easy conversation, the laughter and familiarity was as it had been before they'd met Peter.

After a while, they curled up against each other on the sofa. The softness of Anuli's body was familiar and comfortable.

Anuli tilted her head and brushed her lips against Tessa's. "I've missed you."

"I'm sorry." Tessa sighed.

"You haven't let me touch you since Peter came into the picture." Anuli looked so sad.

Tessa's heart went out to her friend. She had been so engrossed with Peter she hadn't thought that Anuli would feel neglected.

"I didn't mean for it to turn out this way. I just feel as if I should keep myself for Peter. You understand, don't you?"

"I understand, Tessa. But what about me? You have Peter but the only person I have is you. I love you. Don't you know that by now?"

There were tears in Anuli's eyes and they dripped down her cheeks.

A lump clogged Tessa's throat. She'd never seen her friend like this. Almost desperate. Anuli had always been the strong one. The confident one. The one who had slain Tessa's dragons. Yet now, she looked so vulnerable.

Tessa reached across and drew her into her arms, wiping her cheeks. "Do you want me to stop seeing him? Do you want me to cancel our deal with him? I'll do it for you. You know that."

Anuli had been the one who insisted they sign the contract. Although Tessa knew it would hurt to let go of Peter and the money, her friend was more important to her.

"Will you really do it?" Anuli leaned back and looked into Tessa's eyes.

"Yes, if it's what you want. Your friendship is more important to me than the contract or Peter. You should know that."

"I know." Anuli sighed. "I don't want you to cancel the contract. We both need the money. A year is a long time but I'll survive it as long as I know you'll come back to me at the end of the contract."

"I will always be in your life. You can't get rid of me."

"I hope so. Can you do something for me?"

"What?"

"Let me make love to you one last time."

"Anuli—"

"Please don't say no. Please. Just one last time. And I won't disturb you and Peter again."

Tessa puffed out a heavy breath. The idea of having Peter all to herself was enticing. But would Anuli really be okay to leave them to their own devices. "Are you sure?"

"I'm sure. I know the two of you would rather not have me around anyway," the other girl said, brushing hair away from her face.

"Okay. But it's just for tonight."

Anuli's face broke into a smile before she kissed Tessa and pulled her up from the sofa and into the bedroom.

Hours later, she woke in the dark room. Her body was still entwined with Anuli. The other girl had her legs and arms draped around her body. All the lights were off but there was flickering coming from the living room.

Had they left the television on?

Wanting to check, she shifted Anuli's limbs off gently so she didn't wake the other girl. They were both naked, the clothes discarded on the bedroom floor. In the dim light, she managed to find her tunic and pulled it over her head.

She padded into the living room and stopped short when she saw someone lying on the sofa. Her heart thumped hard in her chest.

Peter? When did he get back?

She glanced at the clock on the wall. It was five minutes past four.

How long had he been lying there? She couldn't see his face from this angle so she didn't know if he was asleep or awake.

Why would he sleep on the sofa? It wasn't as if they'd never shared a bed even if they weren't having sex like other people.

Her breath hitched. Had he seen her and Anuli tangled up? Was that the reason he chose to sleep on the sofa? Surely he couldn't have seen them having sex. They would've heard him come into the suite.

What should she do? Should she wake him up?

He'd probably had a long day and a longer journey getting here. She shouldn't disturb him.

She turned back and returned to the bedroom. Tapping the other girl on the shoulder, she woke her.

Anuli stirred. "What is it?"

"Peter is back," she whispered.

Anuli leaned on her elbows. "Where is he?"

"He's sleeping on the sofa."

"Okay. Get back into bed."

"But I don't know when he got back. Do you think he saw us together?"

Anuli shrugged groggily. "It doesn't matter. He knows we're lovers already so it's not a surprise to him if he saw us. Come on. Get back to sleep. You'll see him in the morning."

Tessa climbed back into bed still wearing the tunic. Anuli was back sleeping within seconds but Tessa couldn't get back to sleep.

Peter sleeping on the sofa was not a good thing. She just knew it and she knew the consequences would not be good.

Chapter Fifteen

Peter swung his leg over the side of the sofa. He hadn't gotten much sleep last night. He rubbed his hands over his face before he stood.

The sun was barely up and he could do with a few more hours of snoozing. But he had a lot to do today. This wasn't the time to rest.

Time to get started with his day. He walked over to where he'd left his jacket over one of the dining chairs when he arrived earlier this morning and pulled out his phone. He typed out a message to the hotel manager and sent it.

Then he headed for the bathroom for a quick shower. First, he had to walk through the bedroom with the two women.

He'd seen them when he'd arrived, naked bodies entangled like the lovers they were and the air filled with the scent of sex. Disappointment had made his chest tighten even as his body had curled tight with anger.

He'd stepped away, unable to look at them any longer and needing the distance to calm down and think of what to do. The sleepless night had helped him. Now he had his course of action set.

He walked in the bedroom to find Tessa getting off the bed. "Peter, hi. You're up already."

He didn't stop walking but just gave her a cursory glance. "Yes."

She wore a blue and white linen embroidered tunic and rubbed the back of her neck with her left hand. "I didn't know when you got back last night. I saw you sleeping on the sofa but didn't want to wake you. You should've woken us when you got back."

Her guilt showed in the way she rambled on.

He stopped at the bathroom door and turned to face her. He wouldn't make this easy for her if that was what she was expecting. She stared down at her feet, reminding him of a child who'd been caught doing something bad.

She had done something bad. Although, he'd been resigned to the fact that she would do it. But he hadn't expected to walk in and find them at it on his bed.

He'd bet it had been a deliberate action from Anuli directed at him. She was telling him in no uncertain actions that she had control of Tessa and could do whatever she wanted.

She would soon learn that every action had a reaction. Every deed had a consequence.

"When I arrived the two of you—" he waved his hand from Tessa to the sleeping Anuli and back to Tessa. "—looked too cosy to disturb."

Wide-eyed, her head snapped up as she sucked in a sharp breath and covered her mouth. Her expression confirmed what he already knew.

Heaviness settled on his body and he shook his head as he turned away and walked into the bathroom. Shutting the door, he leaned against the slab and puffed out a heavy breath.

For the uncountable time over the past few hours, he asked himself why he was doing this. Why was he investing time, money and effort in a woman who seemed like a lost cause?

Because you never give up on anything. Because Naaza would be disappointed if you gave up on someone who so obviously needed help.

Because despite everything, he still wanted Tessa. He still wanted to prove to her that there was good out there. That she should stop selling herself short.

To be able to do that, he had to get rid of the biggest influence in her life. Anuli.

There was no way that Tessa would learn for as long as Anuli was still there whispering in her ear like a little devil.

He understood the importance of friendship. After all, he had Michael and Paul. They'd been friends for more than twenty years. But their relationship was based on mutual respect.

What those two had, he couldn't be sure how healthy it was even if it was coming from a good place.

Sighing, he took the clothes he'd had on since yesterday off, tossing them on the cold tiles before stepping into the shower cubicle. He didn't waste time in the shower. Ten minutes later, he was out of the bathroom and went to the closet.

Neither Tessa nor Anuli were in the bedroom. Tessa must have woken her friend which was good because he needed them both awake for what would come next.

He got dressed in a navy linen two piece and navy suede loafers. Then he headed out to the living room.

Tessa and Anuli sat on separate sofas. They looked up and greeted him "good morning."

"Girls, come over here." He didn't want them sitting comfortably for what he had in mind. He pulled out the chair at the head of the dining table and sat down.

Tessa walked over in a hurry, her eagerness to appease obvious. Anuli walked slow, taking her time, her expression one of nonchalance.

Tessa walked a couple of chairs away and pulled one out.

"No," he said and pointed to a spot in front of him. "Come over here."

She hesitated and moved just as Anuli walked around the other side, taking the long route.

"Anuli, you need to come and stand here too."

She eyed him but didn't say anything as she walked over, her movements slow and deliberate. Eventually, she stopped beside Tessa who was fidgeting with the sleeve of her tunic, her gaze averted.

"Do either of you want to sit down?" he asked, keeping his tone steady.

"Yes, of course," Anuli answered as if it had been a stupid question.

He ignored her rudeness. "Sit on the floor."

"What?"

They both stared at him as if he'd lost his mind and stared at the floor.

"You want us to sit in the floor?" Tessa asked, her voice shaky.

"Yes. Right here." He pointed to the spot.

"Why should I sit on the floor when there are chairs all around?" Anuli waved her hand about.

"Because you don't deserve to sit on any of the furniture or use any gadgets in this suite. You're lucky that this floor is carpeted. Have you forgotten that I've been to where you live? Are you trying to tell me that you've never sat on the cold concrete floor in your one-room flat?"

Anuli stiffened, her frown increasing. "That doesn't matter. I'm not going to sit on the floor and you can't make me."

She pulled out a chair and sat on it. Tessa stood where she was as if unsure of what to do.

Peter nodded as he pulled his phone out and pressed the button for Christopher. The man picked the call after the second ring.

"Morning, Chris," Peter responded to his greeting. "Is Tope from the security team on duty today?"

"Yes, he is."

"Good. The two of you should come up to the penthouse."

"Sure. I'll be there shortly."

He hung up and saw Tessa whispering to her friend. "Anuli, please. Let's just sit on the floor. It's not a big deal."

"Ha. I'm not doing it. Anyway, what's his problem? Why are we suddenly sitting on the floor?"

Sighing, Tessa settled on the carpet, pulling her knees up to her chin with her arms around her legs.

"You know exactly why I'm doing this. When this deal began, I told you the rules. And I told you there would be punishment if you disobeyed my instructions."

"Yeah. And?" Anuli countered.

"And I specifically told you that you didn't have permission to have sex with Tessa. Still, I come back to find you two naked and in the aftermath of sex."

"You can't prove anything," Anuli retorted. "People do sleep naked in bed. It doesn't mean they had sex."

"Well, let's find out if it's true or not that you had sex." He turned to Tessa who had been watching their exchange with increasing incredulity. "Tessa, did you have sex with Anuli last night?"

Her brow furrowed and she twisted her lips as she stared from him to Anuli.

"Anuli, did Peter tell you not to have sex with me?" Tessa ignored Peter's question, her face squeezed in a confused frown.

"Yes?" Anuli shrugged.

"When did he tell you?" Tessa sat up, her hands pushing her off the floor as she knelt.

"What does it matter?"

"Answer me, damn it. When did he tell you?" Her hands curled into fists.

"The night we signed the contract." Anuli looked away, fiddling with the placemat.

"So, he gave you specific instructions and you still went ahead to persuade me into it. Why do you keep fighting him? I don't understand you. You're the one who wanted to be part of this deal. You're the one who convinced me to sign the contract. Yet, you're the same one making us antagonise him. Why?"

Anuli shoved the chair back. "Because you belong to me, damn it. Why should he tell me what I can or cannot do with my girlfriend?"

Tessa's mouth dropped open. "What? I'm not your girlfriend. Yes, we're best friends. Yes, we have sex. But we're not dating. I'm not dating anyone. You of all people know that."

"Are you saying you don't love me?" Anuli narrowed her eyes, a scowl on her face.

"Of course, I love you. But I'm not committed to anyone. I don't want to be tied to anyone. I've said that again and again. You are my best friend and that's it."

"So, you don't want to be tied to me. But you will be tied to him for the next year."

"Anuli—"

"Fine. Whatever." Anuli sat back on the chair and turned her back to Tessa.

Tessa sighed dejectedly and turned to face Peter. "I'm sorry, Peter. Yes, Anuli and I had sex last night," she said before pulling her knees back up to her chin.

Seeing her like that tugged at his heart and he was tempted to pick her up. However, he was saved by the knock at the door. Getting up, he headed over and opened the door for Christopher and Tope, letting them in.

"Morning, sir," Tope greeted.

"Thanks for coming, guys," Peter said as he led the men back to the dining area.

Anuli still sat in the chair and Tessa on the floor, although she sat up stiffly when she saw the two men.

"Chris, take Anuli downstairs and introduce her to the rest of the housekeeping team. She'll be working in housekeeping every weekend from now until the date specified in the contract which I sent you a copy."

Anuli leaned back and snorted. "Me working in housekeeping?"

"Yes. The hotel housekeeping team cleans the rooms and the spaces inside the hotel outside of the kitchen, restaurant and lounge. You are now part of the team until the end of our deal."

"Nonsense," Anuli said in a low voice as she stood up. "I'm just going to get my things and leave."

"You can't do that, girl. You owe me a lot of money. If you won't go to housekeeping willingly, then Tope has my permission to lock you up for as long as I wish."

She eyed Tope up and down with disdain. Tope was a huge man—bald head, dark skin, powerful legs and broad shoulders. He instilled fear just by his presence alone. Although you couldn't tell by the look Anuli was giving him.

"He doesn't look like Police," Anuli said, still eyeing Tope.

"He's worse than Police. He's ex-military and he oversees hotel security. There's a guard house on the premises and he can lock you up for as long as is necessary, which can be for the rest of the year."

Michael had recommended Tope to work in the hotel as he'd known the man from his days in the SSS.

"Anuli, please." Tessa stood up in rush. "Go to housekeeping. It's not that bad. It's only for weekends and at least you can come and go freely. Biko."

It was the first time Peter had heard her speak Igbo and she sounded desperate for Anuli's sake.

"Fine. I'll go. But what about you? What is he going to do with you?"

Tessa turned to Peter. "Am I going down to housekeeping too?"

He shoved his hands in his pockets. "No. I have a different punishment for you."

Chapter Sixteen

Tessa hadn't realised how serious Peter had been about the 'special punishment' waiting for her until they had disembarked from a flight to Abuja and were in a car heading to an unknown location.

When Christopher and Tope had arrived in the penthouse, Tessa had known something bad was about to go down. The guy, Tope, had put fear in her heart. He'd looked fierce. That was the only word she could use to describe him.

And when Peter threatened to have the man lock Anuli up, Tessa had really feared for her friend. Anuli was just too damned stubborn for her own good. Tessa had to convince her to go with Christopher.

At least Christopher seemed like a nice man. He'd been cordial even after the debacle with Telema and he'd had a glass of champagne with them after they'd signed the contract with Peter.

The sight of Anuli been marched out of the suite had gotten Tessa agitated again. What would Peter have in store for her? His punishment to Anuli had been harsh but expected in a way since they had been at loggerheads since the beginning.

He hadn't said much to her except to order breakfast. She'd said she wasn't hungry but he'd insisted that she ate. With him sitting right next to her and watching her every move, she'd had no choice but to stuff the food into her mouth and chew, even if she hadn't tasted much of it.

Afterwards, he'd sent her to the bathroom to shower and told her to be out and dressed in ten minutes. When she'd come out of the shower, she'd found her clothes laid out on the bed.

"I want you to wear this." He'd pointed at a long red and black Ankara dress with a tie holding up the bodice round the neck and a flowing maxi skirt.

He'd even picked out the shoes, a matching Ankara platform sandal with diamante sown into the side panels, as well as sunshades.

When she'd finished dressing and looked at her image in the mirror, she looked like royalty, perhaps the countess he'd been calling her previously. He'd stepped up to her from behind, a jewel-encrusted necklace in his hand and placed it on her neck.

Now she fiddled with the necklace nervously, too worried to figure out how expensive it must have been as she sat in the back seat of the Lexus SUV. They drove for an hour on the highway and she wondered if the city of Abuja was very far from the airport. Then they got off the highway and drove for what seemed like another hour on a country road. They were nowhere near a city. All she could see were farms, farmhouses, small towns and villages.

The sun was low in the sky when they pulled up to a large white ranch house that seemed to be in the middle of nowhere. It was surrounded by a high wall and security men opened the black metal gates.

When the car stopped, the driver held the door for them while servants greeted them in a language she couldn't understand and took their bags.

"Welcome, Mr. Oranye," a light-skinned middle-aged woman dressed immaculately in a blue Ankara print dress greeted in a northern accent. "I am Madam Vivian. We've been expecting you. Please follow me."

"Thank you," Peter said and waved a hand for Tessa to follow the woman.

Tessa did and admired the interior design of the house as it was laid out like some of the expensive hotels she'd seen in PHC but also had the feel of being someone's house.

Was this what Peter classed as a punishment? It felt more like one of those exotic holidays she'd read about in romance novels. Still, she couldn't complain. Compared to what Anuli was doing right now, which involved cleaning up other people's messes, she got the better end of the deal from the looks of it.

The woman opened a door and waved them inside. "This will be your room for the night. Everything you requested is in the drawer. Dinner is at seven. I will come back later to take you to the hall."

"Thank you. I'd like to speak to Sir Melaye before dinner, if he's free," Peter said.

"He's free now. If you'd like to come with me," the woman said.

"Wait for me in here," Peter said before walking out and shutting the door.

Tessa looked around the room. It looked like a hotel room with a large four-poster bed at one end and a sofa and small table at the other ends. There wasn't a TV screen. There was electricity as the overhead lamp was on and there was cool air coming from the air conditioner.

Their bags had already been brought in and left on the tiled floor beside the bed. They were obviously going to spend the night here. Why?

Tessa walked over and sat at the edge of the bed. She wasn't sure what to do. How long would Peter be? She got up and walked around before sitting on the low sofa. She rested her head against her arm and must have drifted off to sleep because she was woken when the door opened. She lifted her head.

Peter walked into the room. She sat upright as he settled in the armchair adjacent to the couch.

"I know you're wondering why we're here. This is the time to explain," he said and leaned back in the chair, lifting the ankle of his right leg to rest on the left knee. "Last weekend, you made a promise to keep your body just for me. Last night, you broke that promise by having sex with your friend. By doing what you did, you proved several things to me."

He lifted his hands and counted off the fingers.

"One. You do not keep your promises. Two. You cannot be trusted. Three. You don't understand the concept of fidelity. Four. You have no regards for me or my opinion. And five. You truly are a lost cause."

Tessa flinched as he reeled off the indictments. They were each true and she couldn't refute them. She was guilty of all those things. But hearing him count them off made her cheeks heat and she wished the ground would open and swallow her.

"So, I found myself in a dilemma. Should I give up on something that I truly believe in? Should I let you carry on like nothing's happened, like you haven't insulted and slapped me in the face? I'm a man who doesn't give up easily. I didn't get successful by buckling when things get tough. But I also can't let you think that your behaviour is good. Something drastic needed to happen. So here we are."

He waved his hand to encompass the space.

She held her elbow to her side and crossed her arms over her stomach as a chill ran down her spine. "What do you mean?"

"Coming here is your punishment. Don't be deceived by the looks of things. Everything on the outside looks ordinary. But when you get inside, things start to look different. Right. Not long before dinner. Time to get ready. Stand up and walk over to the mirror."

Her legs trembled as she got off the sofa to do his bidding. The churning in her stomach remained. What could be so bad about going to eat dinner? What kind of food did they serve? She stopped in front of the mirror facing away from Peter.

He came up behind her. "Do you see how beautiful you are in these clothes, with your natural hair styled appropriately and the little make up? You look like the countess you should be. Still..."

He shook his head as if his heart was heavy and burdened. He unclasped the necklace around her neck and removed it, tossing it on the dressing table.

"Still, you will not accept what I give you. You would rather be in the gutter, wallowing with the pigs, rolling in the mud. Well, tonight, you can return to being a whore."

Tessa gasped, her head jerking back. Had she heard him right?

"What did you say?"

"I said, tonight you will become the whore you crave to be. Take your clothes off."

The crassness of his words had her in shock. She didn't move. Just stared at him with her mouth open.

"Take the clothes off, Tessa, or I will rip them off you."

"Okay." Jeez. What was wrong with him? She couldn't believe this was Peter. But she also didn't want him to tear the dress which was lovely and expensive.

She undid the knot at the nape and the ties fell. She unzipped it at the back and pushed the dress down, stepping out of it. Peter picked it up and tossed it on the bed. Next, she unstrapped the shoes and tugged them off.

"The bra and knickers need to come off too," he said as he watched her with an unreadable expression.

Was this about sex? Did he bring her here to fuck her finally?

Sighing, she removed her underwear. He took and threw them on the bed too. Then he opened a drawer and pulled out something that looked like a chunky dog collar. It was made from black leather with a D-ring.

"You are going to wear this as a sign that you belong to me tonight." He buckled it around her neck.

It felt heavy and constricting but soft on her skin at the same time.

He took out a long black leash and hooked it to the aluminium ring at the base of the collar.

Last, he took out a black whole-face mask with holes for eyes and nothing else.

"What is that for?" she asked, feeling even weirder. What the hell was this about?

"This." He lifted the mask. "Is because I'm hoping that underneath all the garbage the call girl is carrying around, there is a countess inside you who will break out one day and thank me for preserving her dignity even in this little way."

"What are you talking about?"

"We're going out to dinner now."

"Okay. I'll find something to wear."

"No. You're coming to the hall with me as you are."

"Naked?" Her eyes felt like it would pop out of the sockets.

"Yes, naked. Tonight, you are my slave. In these premises, slaves don't wear clothes as you'll soon find out. You'll do as you're told and do not think about misbehaving. The owners don't take kindly to slaves who misbehave and I won't be able to help you if you do."

He had to be kidding, right? This was Peter. Clean-cut Peter. Celibate-for-years Peter.

"You're not serious." She laughed nervously. It was ridiculous.

"Why am I not serious? Aren't you a call girl? Don't you sell your body to men for money? What's the point of covering it up with dresses and jewellery? At the end of the day, you'll still be in a strange man's bed, naked and spread out for him to do whatever he wishes. This way, they get to see what they are bidding for exactly as it would be."

"Did you say bid?"

"Oh, yes. I forgot to mention. Sometime during dinner, you'll be put up for auction. The men will bid for you and whoever wins you will spend the night with you. I mean, you don't mind, do you? You said it yourself. You're not committed to me or anybody else. You're happy to go to any man who will pay for you."

Now she knew this had to be a joke. Peter would never let another man touch her. He was the same man who didn't like her dancing with another man in the night club. The whole reason they were here was because she'd slept with Anuli. So, he was never going to go through with this. She would just call his bluff. She could handle it.

"Put the mask on. It's time to go."

She tugged the mask on and it hid her smug smile. She had no problems being naked in front of men. And since she had a mask on, it made it a whole lot easier for her. If he thought he would frighten her by telling her all those things, it wouldn't work.

Let the games begin, Peter. You're not going to win this one.

Chapter Seventeen

Tessa walked two steps behind Peter who led her with the leash connected to her collar. Madam Vivian sashayed in front of them.

It was dark outside as they walked through a corridor that had small spotlights at several intervals on floor level across a courtyard filled with green leafy plants in terracotta pots that gave the place an intimate feel.

Before they arrived at the restaurant, she heard the low vibe of music and conversations. It sounded like the place was busy.

She had her first wave of anxiety as her breathing quickened. How many people were in there? She'd been in an orgy before that involved six people. The sound she heard seemed way more than six people.

And in that situation, she'd had Anuli with her. Now she was on her own without her anchor. Peter who was usually ordinary was behaving strangely.

As they got closer to the door, her heart rate increased. Surely, he'd stop and turn around, saying it had all been a prank to see what she would do.

No. He didn't stop when Madam Vivian opened the door. He walked in.

Breathe, girl. You can do this.

The air was cool as she stepped inside the busy space. There were about twenty people from a rough count. Men in two-piece attires, men in agbada, even two white men in jeans and dress shirts. The men sat in groups of two, three or more around tables.

There were naked women of different shapes and sizes and colour. Some were kneeling on the floor beside the men while others were serving. There was a slim white woman with brown hair kneeling by two men in flowing jalabia.

She'd seen it all now. At least she wasn't alone in her nakedness.

They were led to a table where another man was already sitting. He was a middle-aged man with grey hair in his neatly trimmed moustache and beard. He was a good-looking man in black shirt and trousers and reminded her of Richard Mofe-Damijo. He stood up as Peter approached and shook his hand.

"It's good to have you with us tonight, Peter," the man said.

"Thank you, Sir Melaye. I'm grateful you could fit me in at such short notice."

Peter didn't introduce her as the men sat down. There wasn't a chair for her to sit on and she assumed since some of the other naked women were kneeling, she could kneel too. It beat standing anyway, as she felt the stares from other people on her skin, making it prickle. Her nipples were like bullet tips already from the cool air. Her body went from hot to cold. Sweat beaded on the top of her lip and made her palms clammy.

"Down," Peter said, pointing to a spot beside him.

She lowered herself to her knees. The floor was cold and hard. Shit. Not comfortable. She settled with her bum on her heel, taking the weight off her knees and getting a little comfortable.

How was she supposed to eat from this angle when the tabletop was barely below her head? More to the point, the mask didn't have an opening for her mouth so she couldn't eat without taking it off or at least lifting the bottom. That would mean holding it with one hand while eating with the other from a low angle.

The waiter turned up and took the order from Peter. He didn't ask her what she was going to eat. She'd been told she couldn't speak while she was out here unless someone asked her a direct question. No one asked her any questions.

The men carried on chatting as if she wasn't there. She felt invisible, almost. The first course arrived on a platter. It smelled so nice that her stomach rumbled. Heat flushed her cheeks.

Peter held out a piece of fried shrimp. "Lift the bottom of the mask and eat from my hand."

She felt a little uneasy about being fed as if she were a child or dog under the table. But she was naked in a room full of people. This was just one more thing. It looked like the only way she was going to eat and she was hungry. She hadn't eaten anything since breakfast. The aroma of the spices and herbs made her mouth water. She forgot her unease.

She did as he instructed and he fed her from the platter. On the plus side, the food was delicious. Along with the garlic butter shrimps were avocado slices. For the main course, he fed her pieces of grilled fish and plantain. Occasionally, he let her sip from a glass of water.

Sometime during the meal, a space was cleared at the centre of the restaurant. Two men brought out what looked like a table but it had bars up the sides and steps. It looked like a portable platform. They mounted it in the middle of the room.

A server brought a bowl for Peter to wash his hand. Then Madam Vivian arrived.

"It's time," she said.

"Thank you," Peter said before he reached down and took the collar and leash off Tessa's neck. He placed the items on the table.

"The collar is off, which means you are now available for other interested men. Madam Vivian will take you to the auction block. Best of luck with whoever wins you tonight. I'll see you in the morning for our trip back. Stand up."

Seriously, this was going beyond a joke. She looked up at his face expecting to see a smile. There was none.

"Stand up, Tessa. Don't keep Madam Vivian waiting." Peter's voice hardened.

The woman in question tapped her shoulder as she pushed off the solid floor. Her knees ached and she wasn't sure she could walk properly. Luckily, the woman held her by the elbow and led her to the platform.

"Climb up," Madam Vivian said.

Tessa glanced at Peter, expecting him to call the whole thing off any minute. But he was just looking at her like every other person in the room was watching what was going on.

Tessa climbed the platform. Was he expecting her to beg him not to do this? Why should she? Yes, she'd done something wrong. But this as punishment was just silly, wasn't it? How to punish a call girl? Well, pimp her out to your friends? This was a waste of time, wasn't it? It only reinforced what she was.

He was the one who would miss out if another man bought her.

The woman strapped her to the bars, hands above her head on either side, ankles and thighs spread out and strapped too so she couldn't move.

"Ladies and gentlemen, we have a special specimen today. A newbie you haven't tasted before. We have her in our midst for one night only. Will someone start the bidding at one thousand dollars?"

The table spun slowly so each person in the room could get a good view of her body, front and back.

One of the white men in a black T-shirt raised a white card.

"I have one thousand," Madam Vivian announced.

"Two thousand," someone Tessa couldn't see shouted.

"Three thousand," the white man countered.

"Four thousand," a new voice bid. He was a man in jalabia.

Tessa's heart started thumping hard in her chest. Even with the cold air, she was sweating, her palms turning clammy. This was happening. People were bidding for her. She was on sale, like cattle in the marketplace. Is this what her life had become? She had experienced a few bad things but this had to be on a new level of low.

When she went to the night club every weekend, was this what she did to herself? Did she put herself on a platform and invite people to bid on her?

Yes, it was the same thing. No wonder Peter saw her this way.

Amid it all, she was hoping to hear Peter's voice. Surely, he was going to stop this madness.

Her stomach churned. Her chest tightened. Where was Anuli? She needed her. What would Anuli do? Her friend would tell her to keep her chin up. That these men didn't mean a thing if they had each other.

But they didn't have each other anymore. Things had changed between them. Peter had changed things.

Now she was alone. Without Anuli. Without Peter.

Shutting her eyes, she sucked in a deep breath to quell her panic. She'd survive this. The men didn't mean anything. It didn't matter who won the bidding. It was just sex. She'd done it many times before. She would do it many more times again.

"Sold!" Madam Vivian announced.

Tessa's eyes flew open as she searched for the person who had bought her but she couldn't see any raised cards at this angle. Then two men, the ones who had mounted the platform, stood beside her, untying the straps. Disorientated and confused as she was led down the platform, she twisted her head trying to find Peter but she couldn't.

Where was he?

They led her back out of the restaurant.

"Where are you taking me?" she asked, forgetting that she wasn't supposed to talk.

"You're being taken to your new master's quarters," the woman informed her.

"And who is that?" she asked again.

"You'll find out soon enough. Now no more talking, girl."

She clamped her mouth shut as a man opened the door to a suite that looked larger than the one she and Peter were staying in. The room was dimly lit with just one side lamp.

"Go on. Get on the bed. Abdul, secure her."

The man lifted her onto the bed before she could do anything.

"What's going on?" she asked as she stared from the woman to the man.

"We have to prepare you for your new master. You are a toy for his sexual pleasure."

As Madam Vivian spoke, the man clapped leather cuffs to her limbs and strapped Tessa's arms and legs to the four posters. She was stretched out across the bed. The man went to stand by the door while the woman opened a drawer. She pulled out a tube. She recognised it as containing lubricant. Was the person who bought her not going to bother with arousing her?

Madam Vivian pulled out another object. Tessa also recognised it. An anal plug.

"What do you need that for?" she asked as her heart rate increased again.

"He might want to fuck your ass. This will prepare you." The woman poured gel over the plug and leaned over Tessa.

She tried to wriggle to prevent the plug from going in but she had no movement and the woman shoved the thing into her butt after a few attempts.

Tessa was panting heavily now. "Look. Whoever this person is. I don't want them."

"You cannot change your mind now. He paid a lot of money for you. Ten thousand American dollars. Four thousand is yours. You get it in the morning before you leave."

She was getting four thousand dollars? Anuli would tell her to just relax and collect the money at the end of the day.

But she didn't want the money.

The woman pulled out a blindfold and covered her eyes. She was plunged into darkness.

Shit. Shit. Shit.

She didn't want to be alone with a strange man. She wanted Peter.

"Please, I don't want the money," she shouted. "I want Peter. Please find Peter. Tell him I don't want the money. Tell him I'm sorry."

She heard the door shut and the room plunged into silence.

"Aaaarrrggghhh," she screamed in frustration. What was she going to do now? Would the man who had bought her let her go if she begged?

She tugged at the bonds again but nothing moved.

The door opened and someone walked in. She froze.

"You're a pretty one," the man said. She heard his footsteps as he moved across the room.

Shit. Was he the man in jalabia or the one she couldn't see his face? She tried to place the voice.

If this man fucked her, Peter would hate her. He would think she wanted it to happen. She should've just begged him when he'd first mentioned the auction. She'd never thought he'd let it happen.

Now she was in deep shit.

Chapter Eighteen

Tessa kept perfectly still as she listened out and tried to figure out where the man stood in relation to the bed.

Something light touched her ribs just below the swell of her breast. She shivered.

Shit. He was close. Who was he? He wasn't saying much. But she could feel the burn of his gaze on her skin.

Her heart thumped hard in her chest, blood whooshing loudly in her ears.

"Sir?" Her mouth was dry and she licked her lips.

"Yes, pretty one." His accent was heavy but she couldn't place it.

The object he was using stroked over her breast. The touch was so light, it felt like feathers. Her nipples tightened in response, her breasts grew heavy.

God, no. Her body was getting aroused. She'd expected the person to just take his clothes off and mount her, getting it over with soon. Instead, he was caressing her body with light feathery touches, sending sensation all over her body.

Panting heavily, she panicked. "Sir. Please stop."

He stilled, didn't lift the object though. The tendrils stayed on her left nipple. "What is the matter?" he asked.

"I don't want to do this. I'm sorry."

"Why? You were on the block. I bid and won. I paid a lot of money for you."

She swallowed hard. "I'm sorry, sir. I'll give you back the money. I don't want it."

"You will pay me the ten thousand dollars?"

Shit. She didn't have ten thousand dollars. She swallowed again. "No sir. I only have four thousand dollars. I'll give it to you."

"That doesn't help me, girl. Just relax. You might enjoy this."

Warm, wet mouth covered her nipple. A rough tongue flicked the hard tip. Electricity zipped straight to her clit. A moan ripped from her. Her cheeks burned.

She twisted, trying to get away. More of her breast entered his mouth just as his fingers parted her labia.

"Oh, you are such a slut. Look at how wet you are. You like men using your body." The man stroked her intimately, circling her clit before dipping into her opening.

Her cheeks burned along with her body. Why was her body betraying her like this? She didn't want to respond to this man. She didn't want Peter to hate her.

"Get off me!" she snapped in an annoyed tone.

The man lifted his head from her breast. "Now you're being rude and I won't tolerate it."

He moved away and she heard a drawer opening. Then she felt his heat beside her again.

"Open your mouth," he said in a stern voice.

She refused and he grabbed her cheeks with his hand, squeezing it together. She had no way of fighting him as her hands and legs were still tied up.

"Leave—"

Her words were cut off when he stiffed a ball gag into her mouth and looped it around her head. Now she couldn't see, couldn't talk, couldn't move. She was naked and open, spread-eagled on a bed. This man would be able to do whatever he wanted with her body. She'd never felt so degraded in her life.

"Now. That's what a slut should look like, ready and waiting to be used." The man's words reiterated her thoughts.

There was no one else to blame. She had done this to herself. She had reduced herself to a commodity to be bought and sold. A sex toy to be used again and again.

The man carried on with his ministrations. He touched her body any way he wanted. She was ashamed to admit that her body responded as the man seemed to know what to do to make a woman respond. She was aroused but he didn't let her have an orgasm.

He climbed and entered her, his cock thick and firm as he thrust in and out of her, groaning and grunting. When he came, warm sticky semen splattered all over her stomach.

He got off the bed and left her with his cooling semen on her skin and her body still aroused and uncompleted.

She heard the rustle of fabric. He must be putting his clothes on. Then she heard a *phish* sound that indicated he was sitting on the sofa. After a while, she heard what sounded like soft snores.

He really was going to leave her like this. Hot and sticky, smelling of his cum and sweat while bound, gagged and blindfolded. Never mind that her body was unfulfilled.

Peter, where are you? I'm so sorry. I will never disrespect you again.

He had been trying to save her from all this but she'd thought she knew better. She'd tried to call his bluff. But the joke was on her.

She wanted Peter. He'd told her there were good men and she hadn't believed him. He was a good man and he had been trying to save her. To make her see that she was good and better than a call girl. She could do more with her life. She didn't have to let men use her body.

From the first night she'd met Peter, there had been the undeniable attraction between them. He had protected her and he hadn't asked for anything in return. He had given her money but hadn't asked for sex. He had cared for her and shown her a different side of life. A better side of life.

Before Saturday morning, she'd looked forward to talking to him every night on the phone and had been excited about seeing him again over the weekend. She hadn't known the weekend would end up like this.

She should never have allowed Anuli to convince her to have sex. She'd known it was wrong but she'd wanted to give Anuli one last time together. She'd made up her mind she wouldn't have sex with her friend anymore.

If she hadn't had sex with Anuli, she wouldn't be here right now tied to another man's bed. Perhaps Peter would've been the one making love to her.

Making love. Yes, that's what she and Peter would do. She had a feeling he'd felt very strongly for her. Just like she felt very strongly for him. It had taken for all this to happen before she realised she cared about Peter.

She didn't want to hurt him. But she had been hurting him by going to the night club the other time. That was why he'd paid five million. And she had hurt him by having sex with Anuli. That's why he'd devised this punishment.

Still, she was hurting him now because she hadn't begged him to stop the auction. She'd allowed her foolish pride to lead her astray. Now she didn't know what to do but to take whatever this man dished out.

She drifted off to sleep, feeling low and dirty only to be woken up again in the night. This time, her body didn't respond so readily. She was going to gloat because her body was finally behaving.

He brought out something that buzzed and held it against her clit. A vibrator. *So not fair.*

He forced arousal onto her. Before long, she was writhing and moaning for him. Just when she thought she would come, he stopped. Instead, he came, warm semen splashing all over her chest. Then he left her panting again. She screamed in frustration although the sound was muffled by the gag.

This routine continued all night. He seemed to be waking her every other hour and repeating the same things. He appeared insatiable. And he didn't let her orgasm even once.

She hated this man whoever he was.

He used her like a slave. A sex toy.

The mental and physical torture made her see the truth. Peter had been right about her all along.

"Wake up."

Somebody shook her.

Tessa opened her eyes and blinked a few times at the sunlight in the room. The curtains were open. Her blindfold was off and so was the ball gag.

Madam Vivian stood beside the bed.

Tessa felt so groggy she wanted to curl up and go back to sleep. She moved her hands and legs and nothing restrained her. The straps had been untied.

"Get up, girl. It's time for you to return to Master Peter."

Suppressing a groan, Tessa rolled to her side, expecting to see the man from last night but there was no evidence of him.

"Where is...?" She didn't know his name. Her cheeks flamed. She didn't even know the man who had fucked her body all night that she didn't have the energy to sit upright. "Where is my master from last night?"

"You mean Master Chi? He left early this morning to head to the airport. He has a flight back to Lagos."

Tessa nodded and slowly got off the bed. Her body was caked with dried semen. And she smelled of sex.

"Here, put this on." The woman picked up a robe from the bottom of the bed.

Tessa put it on as quickly as she could, grateful to cover her body. She'd never been so pleased to cover up before. At least she didn't have to walk around naked anymore.

Madam Vivian picked up an envelope from the side table. "Here is your fee for last night. Master Chi was very pleased with you. He left a generous tip."

Tessa's stomach rolled. "A tip? How much?"

"An extra thousand dollars." The woman smiled. "There is five thousand dollars in the envelope."

Tessa recoiled as bile rose in her throat. This had really happened. Another man had fucked her. And paid for the privilege. Peter was going to hate her. Tears built up in the back of her eyes.

"I don't want the money." She stepped away on sore legs.

"Don't be silly, girl. Do you know how hard people must work to earn five thousand dollars? And you want to reject it. Even if you don't need it, don't you have friends or family who can use it?" The woman walked to her and stuffed the envelope in the pocket of the robe. "You've earned the money. You should be proud about spending it."

Tessa swallowed the bitterness in her mouth. She didn't want the money if Peter was going to hate her. Even if she needed it. She needed Peter's approval more.

The woman pulled out a white card. "There are many men who showed an interest in you. If you ever think about coming back here, you will be welcomed. Just call the number on there to book a date. We will cover your travel expense and of course you will earn forty percent of whatever the winning bid on the night." She leaned in close to her ear. "Your Master Peter doesn't have to know that you visited us."

Was this woman serious? She was inviting her back without Peter's knowledge? The idea made Tessa's stomach churn.

"Think about it." The woman put the card in Tessa's pocket too.

"Thank you," Tessa said. She couldn't tell the woman that there was no way she was coming back here again if she had the choice.

Madam Vivian led her out of the room, down a corridor before knocking on a door.

"Come in." She heard Peter's muffled voice.

The woman opened the door and waved Tessa in. She walked in and the door shut behind her.

Her heart raced as she stared at Peter sitting on the armchair with his back in her direction. Then he stood up and turned around to face her. He looked immaculate as always in a white shirt and blue jeans. She'd missed him. Missed seeing him. Missed being in his arms.

She had never ached for any other person the way she ached for him. She'd never felt this strongly about Anuli. She was in love with Peter.

His grim expression said he wouldn't be pulling her into his arms anytime soon.

"Peter—" she started but he cut her off.

"Go into the bathroom and clean up. You stink of sex." He walked around and past her to the door. "Be washed and dressed by the time I get back. I've left you the clothes to wear."

He pointed at the bed where clothes were laid out and then he was gone.

Her heart sank. She'd found the one good man and had fallen in love. But it was too late.

Chapter Nineteen

Peter sat silently in the car, lips pressed together in a grimace. They were on the way from the airport to the hotel in PHC. They'd left Richa Ranch hours previously to drive back to Abuja airport and then take the flight to Port Harcourt City.

He glanced at Tessa. She had her eyes closed with her head leaning towards the window. He wasn't sure if she was asleep. But she'd slept during the drive to Abuja and on the plane, evidence that last night had taken its toll on her physically. Whether there was an emotional and psychological impact was yet to be determined.

He'd agonised all last night about whether the events of the night would be effective. Whether he'd made the right decision in taking her to the ranch and putting her through the trial by Richa. Would she learn the lessons or would it be business as usual on planet Tessa?

Of course, he'd put himself through an ordeal too by letting it happen.

Right from the moment he'd told her to take her clothes off in the bedroom, he'd hoped that something inside her would snap and she would tell him to go to Hell. That she'd felt no shame in walking naked into a restaurant full of people had appalled and impressed him in equal measures.

Yes, there'd been other bare women there and Tessa had a mask on. But he'd expected her to have a sense of self. A sense of shame. She'd felt none. Shown none.

Even as she'd been led onto the platform to be auctioned, he'd hope she'd tell him to stop it. She hadn't. Instead, she'd stared at him boldly as if daring him. As if it was nothing to her.

It had been then he'd realised he would have to see this through. She hadn't learnt anything yet.

So, he'd sat through the whole ordeal of watching other men ogle her naked body as if she was displayed for their amusement. For their pleasure.

He'd listened as they'd bidden for her, the price climbing higher and higher.

He'd prayed as the price had gone up, waiting for the moment she would shout 'stop'. Then he would step in and rescue her, cover her up and promise her she would never have to put her body up for sale again.

Instead, the hammer had come down.

Sold.

It had gone out of his hands then. He couldn't save her anymore.

No one could save her. She had to go through the full experience and hopefully see herself as everyone else saw her. Only then could she save herself.

It had been one of the most difficult decisions he'd made in his life. And he was a man used to making difficult choices especially with his businesses. But he'd felt the stakes had been too high with this one.

He didn't want to analyse too much why he was so hung up on a woman who on the face of it wasn't right for him on so many levels. Was he just doing it so he could tell himself that he'd tried? Of course not. There was more to it. He cared about Tessa. More than he'd cared about any woman since Naaza.

And that was the scary thing. Tessa was so different from Naaza. If he wanted to find a new love in his life, shouldn't he be looking at women who bore characteristics close to that of his late fiancée?

He scrubbed both hands over his face and shook his head softly. He was driving himself insane for a woman who through her actions had proven she didn't care about him.

Horse, water and drink came to mind and his lips curled in a wry smile.

Please, let it all be worthy.

He glanced at Tessa again. Aside from her obvious exhaustion, he couldn't tell if it had worked. He had to wait to find out.

The waiting tightened his chest and made his body heavy with conflicting emotions. He had a headache and could really do with some sleep. He closed his eyes.

Before long, the car pulled under the portico of the hotel entrance. The doorman opened the car door. Peter stepped out just as the driver opened the other door for Tessa.

Peter waited for her by the sliding doors as their bags were offloaded from the car. They walked side by side into the lobby and across to the lift. The receptionist welcomed them and he waved at the man.

Inside the lift, his weariness caught up with him. The light floral scent of her perfume filled his nostrils. The urge to pull her into his arms increased. He'd missed her. Missed the easy conversations they'd had during the week. Missed the softness of her body when they were cuddled up.

Inhaling deeply, he closed his eyes. If he gave in so quickly, then this whole weekend would've been a waste of time, energy and money.

The lift pinged. He opened his eyes as the doors slid apart.

Time to examine the weekend and find out if it had been a disaster.

He unlocked his suite and waved Tessa inside. She entered but didn't go far in. She stood by the dining table. He walked past her into the bedroom. In the closet, he pulled out his travel case and started packing what he needed for his trip back to Enugu.

He heard a knock on the door and a few seconds later voices before the door shut.

Tessa appeared at the door of the bedroom with the bags. "It was just the concierge with our bags."

"Okay. Just put mine on the floor," he said.

She dropped the bag but remained standing by the door. "Are you going somewhere?"

He glanced up at her. "It's Sunday afternoon. I must head back to Enugu. You know I don't like to be on the roads too late."

"Oh, I forgot about that." She sounded disappointed.

"Yeah. Well, it's been a busy weekend for everyone."

"About that. I want to apologise for what I did with Anuli. I'm sorry for breaking my promise to you and abusing your trust. I know it's probably too late to say it now but I realised my mistakes and I won't do them again."

He straightened and shoved his hands into his pockets so he didn't reach for her. Was she being genuine with her apology or was she just saying what she thought he wanted to hear?

"Okay. I accept your apology. But if I'm honest, I don't know if I can trust you, Tessa. I don't know that you won't go back to doing whatever you want to do the minute I get in the car and head for Enugu."

Her throat rippled as she swallowed and her eyes glistened. She nodded. "I know. You have no reason to trust me. I screwed up pretty bad this weekend. But I'd like the chance to show you that I've changed. Can I come back next weekend?"

He tilted his head. "I'm not going to be here next weekend."

She squeezed her eyes shut and tears seeped through the corners and dropped on her cheeks.

"You hate me. I knew it." She choked and slumped against the post.

His chest tightened and he found it difficult to breathe. "Tessa, I don't hate you."

She lifted her head and blinked. "You don't?"

"I don't. Come here." He opened his arms.

She stumbled across the room and fell into his arms, sobbing. He lowered his body onto the edge of the bed and pulled her onto his lap. She gripped his shirt, her face on his chest as she continued to cry. He let her cry for as long as she wanted. He'd learned that tears were cleansing and healing. She needed to shed them as much as he'd needed to see her shed them.

They stayed holding each other for minutes until she quietened. Then he reached for his handkerchief and wiped her face.

"Do you really have to go to Enugu tonight?" she asked in a low voice when she leaned back a little.

"I have a couple of meetings scheduled for tomorrow."

"Oh." She sounded so small. So disappointed.

"I thought you had things to do tomorrow. You specified you weren't available Mondays to Fridays."

She shrugged. "I thought maybe you could leave in the morning."

"My first meeting is at nine a.m. I won't have any leeway if I leave in the morning. And I don't like being late for anything even when I'm the boss. Especially when I'm the boss."

She nodded sadly. "I understand."

Just seeing her downturned features had him rethinking. "I can have my meetings tomorrow through video or teleconference, so I don't have to be physically there."

She perked up. "You can?"

"Yes. I just need to get it arranged. I'll send my assistant an email to arrange it on the Enugu end and I'll check with Christopher to make sure that one of our meeting rooms is free downstairs. Worst case scenario I can have the meeting using the webcam on my laptop."

"You'll do this for me?" She appeared incredulous.

"Of course, Tessa. In case you haven't figured it out yet, I care a great deal about you. I want to spend as much time as possible with you." He tugged her chin up to make eye contact.

"Even after I ruined your weekend?" She had tears in her big amber eyes again.

"Well, I hope you're going to make up for it." He smiled at her.

"Yes, I will. I want to, so much." Her face brightened as she blinked.

"So, we'll spend tonight together and you can start making it up to me." He winked at her.

Her lips curled in a slow smile. "I don't deserve your kindness and forgiveness but I'm very grateful for a second chance."

"We're both learning. We'll work it out."

He leaned forward and brushed his lips against hers. She sighed and went pliant against him. Her soft lips opened when he slipped his tongue into her warm depth. He couldn't resist the groan that rumbled inside him.

She tasted so good. He hadn't kissed her all weekend. Now all the emotions that had been bottled up inside him loosened and poured into the kiss, translating into passion.

He forgot everything else, his misgivings, his anger, his frustrations, his concerns and got lost in Tessa. In her taste. Her warmth. Her softness.

He lowered her onto the bed and covered her body with his. He lifted his head and gazed into her amber eyes. His heart raced and beat so hard, he felt it would punch a hole in his chest.

"Peter, about last night—"

"Shh." He quietened her. He didn't want to remember what he'd done. He didn't want it to taint this moment. He trailed kisses down her chin to her neck.

"I need you, Tessa." He bared his soul to her. "I need you like I haven't needed anyone in a long time. Will you let me in? Will you let me fill the emptiness inside your heart?" He placed his palm on her chest above her left breast, feeling the thump of heartbeats.

Her throat rippled and she licked her lips before nodding. "Yes, Peter. I need you too."

He lowered his hand, sliding over the swell of her breast, down to her soft tummy to the junction of her thighs. He cupped her pussy through her dress.

"Will you welcome me inside you?"

"Yes, Peter. Please make love to me." She reached up and wrapped her arms around his neck and kissed him hard. She set his body ablaze.

He broke the kiss. "God, Tessa. You are going to drive me crazy."

Her smile was a mixture of sweet and coquettish.

"Sit up," he instructed as he shifted and grabbed the hem of the dress to pull it over her head. She lifted her hips and he tugged it over her waist and the rest of her torso. He tossed it aside, revealing her bra which she was already unhooking. It fell apart, baring her full breasts. He reached for them, cupping them, rolling the tips with his thumbs.

"You are so beautiful." His voice was thick and rough.

He loved her curves and wanted to trace and mould every inch of them. Her skin was warm and smooth and soft. She moaned as he worked her breasts, arching her body into his touch.

Warmth spread through his body just watching and touching her. His cock pulsed in his jeans. He was going to have to free himself soon and sink into her. But first, he wanted her to cry out his name. He'd missed the sound of her orgasms.

He cupped her pussy again though her lace panties. Her heat scorched him through the fabric even as he felt the wetness. He slipped his hand beneath the undie and stroked her pussy.

She mewled, her thighs falling apart.

He separated her labia, circled her clit and then tugged it. She let out a long moan and canted her hips.

"Peter, please..."

He stroked her skin. It would be hypersensitive. A caress here, a pinch there and her orgasm came with a long scream of his name. He kept stroking until her body bowed off the bed and writhed in wave after wave.

Then he ripped off his clothes in record time, unable to hold himself back. He undid his belt and zipper and shoved his jeans down along with his boxer briefs and kicked off his shoes. His rigid shaft sprang free and jutted straight towards her. He only undid two of the buttons of his shirt and pulled it off over his head. Reaching for his wallet, he took out a foil of condom he'd put there specifically for this moment with her and rolled it on.

Then he knelt between her widened thighs. Cock in hand, he nudged her entrance. He put his hand under and lifted her ass while rubbing the head of his cock around her slick folds.

"Tell me what you want."

"Peter, fill me with you." His name on her lips was orgasmic. Her voice so sexy that it was like velvet over his skin. Her hair lay tousled over the sheet, creating a kind of untidy halo.

His cock throbbed. He couldn't hold back any longer. With a hard push, he slammed into her. He held still as her walls rippled around him, her body still in orgasmic throes.

She wrapped his legs around his hips. He fought not to come so soon and gulped in air as she opened her eyes and looked up at him. Her eyes were hazy with lust. Her tongue darted out and licked her bottom lip. She gave him a lazy smile. Her breasts bounced with his movements.

He leaned down and kissed her again, infusing it with raw sexual hunger as his hips started moving and he pistoned into her welcoming wet heat. He slid out slowly and rammed in hard.

Wiggling, she clung onto him as her fingernails dug into his back. He welcomed the pain as she marked his skin. He mixed plain old hard fucking with gentle and tender caressing, alternating the two.

Her tongue teased his mouth as she dipped in and out of him. He let her play with him for a while. It was fun being the recipient of her teasing.

Eventually, he changed it up, making the kiss more demanding as his own needs took over. He nipped her lips, top and bottom. Nipped the line of her chin.

Her eyes were bright and twinkled. Her lips were lush and parted and she panted.

His basic urges took over and he lost control. He lifted her left thigh so he could deepen his thrusts into her as he drew a pebbled nipple into his mouth.

Her muscles clenched around him, her body hungry and yielding. She whimpered and shut her eyes. He felt the tremors that indicated she was close to a climax. He wanted to come with her this time around.

Sweat dripped down his back as he withdrew and pushed back into her clenching channel again and again until he felt the fire build up in his balls. She fell into her orgasm and pulled him right into one, clasping him in tight slick heat as she moaned again.

His mind spun and his eyes rolled back. He thrust one last time and spilled into the condom.

Chapter Twenty

"So, you know I'm not going to be here next weekend," Peter said as they sat in the large tub later.

"Why?" Tessa sat between his spread legs with her back to his chest. Warm water and bubbles that smelled like coconuts surrounded them. He squeezed the sponge and rubbed it over her skin in a leisurely pace.

"Paul, one of my best friends, is getting married in two weeks. Technically, he's already married since he did a registry wedding. But it's his traditional wedding coming up. Anyway, his bachelor's party is next weekend in Barcelona."

Tessa smiled. "It sounds like fun."

"It should be. We leave on Thursday and get back sometime on Monday."

"You're going to have to tell me all about it when you get back and take lots of photos. I'd love to see what Barcelona looks like. Apart from where we went yesterday, I've never been anywhere else."

His mouth dropped open. "Not even to Aba or Owerri or Enugu?"

"Nope. None of those places."

"We're going to rectify that soon. You're coming to Paul's wedding with me."

She twisted around to look at him with bulging eyes because he'd lost his mind. "You want to take me to your friend's wedding? Are you crazy? Have you forgotten what I am?"

"You're not that anymore, and I want you to stop thinking like that. You and me, we're trying out a committed relationship, aren't we?"

A smile bloomed on her face. "Yes."

"And that means we're dating."

"We're dating?" Her smile got wider.

"Yes, as of tonight. It's official. You're my girlfriend."

"I like the sound of being your girlfriend."

"Good. So as my girlfriend, will you be my plus one and accompany me to the wedding of Paul Arinze and Ijeoma Amadi?"

"Yes. I would love to be your plus one." With a huge grin on her face, she twisted around and planted a kiss on his lips. Her heart was so full of joy it felt like it would burst. She couldn't think of a time she'd been happier.

She caressed her hand over his pecs as she broke the kiss and slid her hand lower to cover his erection.

He gripped her hand. "Countess, I don't want to make you sore. So be a good girl and sit back down so we can finish soaking in the bath."

She huffed in a mock tantrum and he chuckled. She giggled and turned around to sit back down.

"Will you tell me how you met Anuli?" he asked.

On the journey back to Port Harcourt, she'd debated about telling Peter about her past and had concluded that if she would earn his trust again, she had to reveal some if not all the details of her past.

Anuli was the only one who knew and she'd also made the decision to cool her relationship with her friend and keep it platonic between them. With Anuli out of the way, she could focus her attention on Peter.

She'd hoped she would get some time to tell him if not this weekend then next time. But he'd already indicated he wouldn't be in PHC next weekend, so this was as good a time to share some of her past.

Even with the decision, thinking about the past still left her uneasy.

She swallowed a couple of times and cleared her throat before speaking.

"I met Anuli for the first time when I was about fourteen years old. She was sixteen. A man I knew as Uncle Joe brought her to our house. I later found out that Anuli's mother had married Uncle Joe but her mother died. Uncle Joe wasn't Anuli's father. At the time, I found it quite difficult fitting in with children of my age especially in school. I wasn't allowed to make friends. Anuli and I got along almost instantly. We were two misfits who seemed to understand each other and we fit well together. We've been inseparable ever since."

It wasn't the entire story but it was a start and she wasn't keen to go into the rest.

"Did you grow up in PHC?" Peter asked, stroking down her arms gently.

"No. I was born in Okigwe and I lived there until Anuli and I moved to Port Harcourt seven years ago."

"Just the two of you?"

"Yes." She shifted uncomfortably. This was bordering on a topic she didn't want to discuss.

"Hang on. That would mean you were sixteen years old when you came to live here and Anuli was eighteen. Just the two of you. What about your parents and her stepfather?"

She crossed her arms and uncrossed them. "I didn't really know my mother. I was a baby when she died. It was me and my father for a long time."

"Where you close to your father?"

She swallowed and pulled her legs up. Her voice shook as she spoke. "In... In a sense." Her whole body started shaking.

He must have detected something was wrong, because he leaned forward and turned to look at her face. "What's the matter? If you don't want to talk, you don't have to."

"No. Peter. You need to know this about me. You need to understand why I'm the way I am. I don't want to ever disappoint you again."

He pulled her into a quick hug. "Okay. Let's get out of the water and get dressed. Then you can tell me the rest."

"Alright."

He stood up and helped her get out of the bath before they wrapped up in robes. He took her hand and they walked out into the living room. On the sofa, he pulled her up between his thighs.

When she was comfortable, she started speaking again.

"The reason Anuli and I came to live in PHC is because we ran away from home."

He froze for a few seconds. "Wow. Ran away? Why would you do that at such a young age too?"

She turned around to face Peter. She had to look into his eyes and see his reaction when she said this. Because she knew her future self-worth would depend on his response to what she was about to say.

She sat rigidly, twisting the tips of the sash in her hand. "We ran away because we were being abused. Me by my father and Anuli by Uncle Joe."

He stiffened, eyes going wide. "What the hell? Hang on. By abused, you mean they were hitting you."

Her scalp prickled as she shivered. She shook her head slowly. "Sex...sexually. It—it wasn't just the two of them. But they were the leaders."

"Your father? Oh, my goodness." The light in his eyes died and he pulled her into a tight hug and held her for long minutes. It was as if he didn't want to let her go.

"I'm so sorry. I'm so sorry." He sounded broken.

She lifted her head and looked into his eyes. She couldn't believe he was apologising. He hadn't done anything wrong. "Why are you sorry? You had nothing to do with it."

His eyes were dull and his face downturned. "I wish I could've saved you from those men. I want to kill those men, Tessa. If I ever meet them, they are dead."

Tessa shuddered and closed her eyes. "Please, I'd like to forget about them. Is it okay if we don't talk about it anymore?"

"Of course. Whatever you want." He pulled her back into his arms.

She sank into him and exhaled a long sigh. "Thank you."

Chapter Twenty-One

Peter stayed in PHC until Wednesday, working from his hotel suite. He had his meetings via video and telephone. The rest of the time, he worked on his laptop.

Tessa had gone into school briefly on Monday, stopped by her residence to pick up her books and returned to Peter's penthouse suite for the rest of the time. It was revision week as she had exams next week. While Peter worked, she studied. In between, they ate food from room service and made love any chance they got.

Like with everything else he did, Peter was an attentive, generous lover and he worshipped her as if she were the countess he nicknamed her. Afterward, they would cuddle up and he would talk about his family and friends fondly. He was a man surrounded by love.

He also talked about his late fiancée. She had been his first love. His one love. Her death had devastated him so much he hadn't been with another woman since. Until Tessa.

An ache bloomed in her throat for his loss. She squeezed him tight as he talked about the woman he'd loved, Tessa giving him comfort the way she could.

Surprisingly, he said that Naaza would have liked Tessa. She'd been a radical lawyer with a passion for human rights. She had advocated for awareness on women's rights and issues.

Tessa admitted to him that she would've loved to meet Naaza. She would've liked to meet the woman who Peter had loved so she could learn what Peter loved in the woman and perhaps replicate it in some way.

As she listened to Peter, she wondered if any man could love her the way Peter had loved Naaza. It was wishful thinking. No man could possibly love her totally and unconditionally, not with her past. Not with the things she'd done.

But if Peter cared for her a little, she would take it with both hands and cherish it. It was more than any man had done for her.

During her time with Peter, Tessa tried to chat with Anuli a few times and called her phone. Anuli hadn't picked the calls. She even sent a text message which remained unanswered.

"While I'm gone, stay in the suite," Peter said as he got ready to head back to Enugu on Wednesday afternoon.

"Here? By myself? It's not necessary," she replied, surprised he would suggest it and not keen on being in the spacious suite alone.

"I think it is. You've got exams next week and I would rather you stayed here to study and prepare. At least you won't have to worry about power cuts and heat waves. You can study at any time you want. You also don't have to worry about cooking food or spending your money buying food. I was a student once so I know the drill." He grinned at her.

"You have a point. Okay, I'll stay." Her smile faded and she scrubbed her foot on the carpet. "Can I ask a favour, please?"

He was packing away his laptop and glanced up at her. "Sure."

"It's about Anuli. I've been trying to reach her all week but she's not taking my calls. If I stay here alone, I'd feel as if I was abandoning her and I really don't want to do that no matter what has happened."

Sighing, he straightened. "Would you like her to stay with you?"

"Well, yes. If you don't mind. I know she's been difficult to you and I won't blame you for saying no. She is still my friend. I don't want to give up on her."

He tugged her hand and pulled her into his arms. "I wouldn't want you to give up on her either. But you must know your limits and keep to them. Don't let her push you into anything you don't want to do. I will have to trust you to do what's right in my absence."

Tessa puffed out a relieved breath. "I won't break your trust. Thank you. Honestly, I don't know if she'll come."

"Oh, I'm sure she'll want to get one over on me when she finds out I'm away. But I've got Christopher and Tope briefed and they know what to do if she causes trouble. If you need them, I've left their contact details on the table. Store them on your phone for emergency even when you're out of the hotel. Okay?"

"I will. Thank you. But there's no need to worry. All I'm doing is wake, bathe, eat, study, sleep for the rest of this week. All my attention is on passing my exams. So, you can be sure there's no danger of me getting into trouble."

"Yes, I'm hoping the week passes sedately for you. But I won't discount anything where Anuli is concerned so the help is there if you need it."

After Peter left, Tessa tried Anuli's number again but got no response. She assumed the other girl was also studying in preparation for the exams so she chose not to disturb her again until she heard back.

When no response came by Friday afternoon, she headed home. They were both doing one year pre-degree programmes at the University of Port Harcourt but in different courses so they didn't sit in the same classes.

Tessa spent the night alone and was woken up on Saturday morning by Anuli as she stumbled into the room early in the morning.

"Where have you been all night?" Tessa asked as she sat up in bed.

Anuli gave her a disdainful look as she slumped into the wooden reading chair next to the desk and pulled off her shoes. "Where else? I went to work of course."

"Work? You don't clean rooms at night at the hotel," Tessa countered. Peter had explained the work Anuli was supposed to do and it was a day job that started at eight in the morning and ended at four in the afternoon.

"Of course, I didn't go to do that shitty job," Anuli said as she stood and shimmied out of her clingy red dress.

"You went to the night club." Tessa's heart sank.

"Not the one you think. I went to our old hang out in Woji. Bagged two white men. I've been with them all night long."

She pulled out a wad of cash from her bag, waved it in the air before unlocking the small box they stored cash in prior to banking it. She locked the box and hid it under the dirty pile of clothes in the closet and put the key in her bag.

Tessa's body went cold and her limbs became heavy. Peter had been right. Anuli hadn't learnt anything even with her punishment. It seemed she was even more determined to ruin her life.

"Why are you doing this to yourself? Do you want to keep selling your body to men?"

"What is the alternative?" Anuli snapped. "That I lie down and take whatever a man will do to my body. That I give it away for free? At least this way, I get compensated for it."

"But it can be different."

"No. It can never be different for me. Do you know how long men have been using my body? I barely had any breasts when Uncle Joe was lining them up to touch me up, damn it. Have you forgotten?" Anuli turned away and slammed her hand on top of the desk.

Everything on the table jumped. Tessa flinched at the loud noise as the back of her eyes burned. She wrapped her arms around her stomach.

"I haven't forgotten," Tessa replied in a constricted voice. "I'm sorry. I didn't mean to upset you."

Anuli sighed and pulled her sleep shirt from the drawer and put it on. Then she climbed into the bed beside Tessa.

"Look, I'm glad you met a nice man. Although I give him a hard time, Peter isn't all that bad. I like that he treats you well. And as long as he keeps treating you well, I'm happy for you."

"You are?"

"Of course, I am. You more than anyone I know deserves some happiness and if Peter can give it to you then I have to let him. All I've ever wanted was for you to be happy. You know that, right?"

"I do."

"Good. Now I need some sleep. You know these white men. They like to fuck every hole available. Mehn, I'm tired." She pulled the sheet up over her body.

"Are you seriously not going to work at the hotel today?" Tessa asked, still hoping her friend would see the light.

"Nope." She turned on her side away from Tessa.

"Peter won't be happy when he finds out."

"Like I care what he thinks."

"But I guess I can get you the time off since he's away this weekend."

Anuli lifted her head and glanced back at Tessa. "He's away? Where's he gone?"

"To Barcelona. One of his friends is getting married. It's the stag party this weekend."

"No wonder you're here." Anuli settled back in bed.

Tessa got out and took her phone from her bag. She dialled the number for Christopher that she had saved earlier.

"Hello," the man answered.

"Good morning, Mr. Christopher. This is Tessa."

"Hi, Tessa. How are you?"

"I'm well, thank you. I'm calling you on behalf of my friend Anuli. I don't know if Peter told you already but we have exams next week and we're doing revisions now."

"Yes, Peter mentioned something about exams."

"Good. I just wanted to ask for some time off for my friend Anuli. We're both doing revisions. Would it be possible to give her some time off today and tomorrow? I'm sorry for the short notice but I'll really appreciate it if you could help us out."

"Of course, Tessa. I will get someone else to cover for your friend. I hope to see her back when the exams are over. My best wishes to both of you on your exams."

"Thank you very much, sir. I appreciate it."

"Don't mention it. Have a nice day."

"Same to you."

Tessa hung up, feeling a bit better. She knew Christopher had only agreed because of Tessa's relationship with Peter. Another positive impact of having Peter in her life. People willing to do favours for her.

"Nuli, the manager agreed to give you time off for your revisions and exams."

The only sound that came from her friend was snoring. Tessa sighed.

At least Anuli would have time off with permission so she wouldn't get into trouble. Hopefully, Tessa would be able to persuade her to go back to work after the exams.

Chapter Twenty-Two

"Are you sure you don't want to come along?" Anuli asked later that evening as she pulled on her purple platform heels. She was dressed in a strapless stretchy dress that showed off her curves.

"No way." Bile rose in Tessa's mouth at the thought of going on the prowl, hunting for men who would pay to have sex with her. Now watching her friend get ready, Tessa shuddered at the knowledge she had once been a part of this weekend ritual. "I'm going to head back to Park Hotel. Why don't you come with me? We can chill out a little, eat food while watching movies. That way, we'll be refreshed to do more studying tomorrow. Come on, please."

"I'm not going back to the hotel. If they see me, they'll want me to work tomorrow," her friend replied, picking up her bag and checking the contents.

She took out the extra packs of condom from the drawer and shoved them inside as well as a small tube of lubricant. They always made sure they had the supplies ready in case the men were not prepared.

"I already told you the manager gave you the weekend off work so you can study. And if you come back to the hotel with me, Peter would know that you were studying because I would be your alibi."

"But I don't want to study tonight. I want to party."

"So, we don't have to study. As I said, let's watch movies and chill out. We can study tomorrow."

"But I want to party tonight. Why don't you come with me to the club and afterwards we can go back to the hotel? We don't even have to pick up any men. It can be just the two of us having fun."

Tessa shook her head. "I can't. I told Peter I would just chill out this weekend."

"Then don't tell him you went to a night club."

"I can't do that. I promised I won't lie to him anymore."

"Then don't tell him any lie. Just tell him that you decided to go the club and afterwards we went to the hotel."

Tessa started pacing the short space of the room. "That's even worse. The minute I tell him I went to the night club, he'll think I was with another man. I can't have him think of me like that. I'm not that girl anymore."

Anuli grabbed her arm, stopping her movement. "Well, he's going to have to trust you. Otherwise, what is the point of your relationship?"

"Ha." Tessa gave a bark of laughter. "You want him to trust me. After everything we did to him.

Not to mention what I did at the ranch he took me to."

"Yeah, how is that your fault? He's the one who took you to the ranch as punishment." She did air quotes with her fingers. "He's the one who put you up for auction. He can't then complain if someone else buys you and fucks you. So, you called his bluff and you earned five thousand dollars. I see that as a win for you."

Tessa growled in frustration. "Did you not hear a word I said about that? Did I not tell you that I felt dirty and degraded afterwards? That I was disgusted with myself when I had to go back to Peter while my body was aching and smelling and caked with another man's semen. I never want to put myself through that again."

Anuli rolled her eyes. "That's what you say. But you still got five thousand dollars and you and Peter are all made up now. So, as I said, you won."

"This is not about winning or losing."

"Yeah. Whatever. All I'm saying is that Peter should trust you. You've told him you won't be with other men. He should accept it. Otherwise, if you watch your step all the time and only do the things he wants, then it's another form of slavery. And remember, we ran away from all that. You don't want to put yourself in that kind of situation."

The implication of Anuli's words made Tessa angry. She snapped and shoved Anuli. "Don't say that crap about Peter."

Anuli reared back. "It's like that, now? You're defending Peter and you want to fight me? Is that it?"

Tessa glared at her. "I don't want to fight you. But Peter is nothing like my father or Uncle Joe. You can't compare him with those disgusting men. He has never treated me the way they did. And I resent that you would think he's like them."

"Okay o." Anuli lifted her hands in the air. "I give up. I'm now the devil while Peter is the saint. Don't come crying to me when everything crumbles around you."

Her friend picked up her bag, yanked the door open and stormed out.

"Anuli, wait." Tessa ran after her. "I'm sorry for shouting."

Her friend brushed her pleas away and kept on walking.

Downtrodden, Tessa returned to the room, packed her things and returned to the hotel.

When Peter called that night, she told him about the bust up with Anuli. He tried to console her on the phone and it soothed her for a little bit. But Anuli remained on her mind for the rest of the weekend.

On Monday, she was in school for her first exam paper. Although her mood had been soured by the argument with her friend, she did her best on the English exam and hoped to get a good result.

As she walked out of the exam hall, one of the students approached her. "Tessa, you are requested at the Dean Preye's office."

"Me? Why?" She'd never had any problems in school and never had any reason to be summoned before the dean.

"I don't know." The student shrugged. "He said you need to report to his office immediately. I think there was a man with him." The girl walked off.

A man? Tessa couldn't figure out who it would be. Had Peter arrived back to Nigeria already and decided to pay her a visit? She didn't know any other men who knew of her studies at this university apart from Peter. Unless it was Christopher or Tope. But why would they come here.

Oh no! Had something bad happened to Peter? God please no. She ran, hurrying to get to the office and find out what had happened.

"I'm Tessa Obum," she told the dean's assistant. "I was told to come here."

"Yes," the woman replied. "Dean Preye is waiting for you. Go straight through."

"Thank you," Tessa said and knocked on the door leading into the dean's office.

"Come in," a male voice said from the other side.

She turned the handle, pushed the slab open and stepped in.

Her heart stuttered in her chest and a cold finger of dread slithered down her spine.

Dean Preye sat in his chair at the other side of the desk. But it wasn't him that got Tessa's attention. It was the man sitting on one of the guest chairs, with his body turned to look at who had arrived.

Telema George.

What was he doing here? He had a smug grin on his face as if he knew something she didn't. How did he find out about her school? She always made sure to keep her school life separate from her work as a call girl. She even went as far as changing her appearance every Friday and Saturday night so people wouldn't recognise her afterwards.

Tessa's heart thumped so hard, she thought everyone in the room could hear it.

"Come in and sit down, Miss Obum," the dean said and waved to the spare seat.

Tessa walked tentatively to the chair and sat down gingerly, making sure not to make any contact with Telema.

"This is Mr. George. He is an alumnus of this great university and we're proud to have him visit us today," Mr. Preye said in the way of introduction. "Mr. George, this is the young lady we have been discussing?"

Telema nodded but didn't say anything.

What the hell was going on? What had they been discussing about her? She never caused any trouble in school and her attendance to classes was almost, if not, one hundred percent.

"Sir, what is this about?" she asked as her skin prickled under the stare of both men.

The dean coughed and leaned his arms on the desk. "It has been brought to my attention that something is wrong with your registration here at our esteemed institution. It is alleged that you are here under false pretences."

Shit. She was in big trouble. Her legs bounced off the floor as her body trembled.

When she and Anuli ran away, they couldn't take any identity details with them like birth certificates because they had been in a hurry. When they got to Port Harcourt and they started earning some money, Tessa wanted to go back to school because she'd missed so much. But she couldn't because she didn't have any ID.

In the end, they'd had to get a fake ID card printed for her when she turned eighteen. She'd changed details of her name and state of origin so that she couldn't be traced back to her old home in Okigwe.

"We do not tolerate such things in this school. You are suspended with immediate effect, pending further investigations. You should note that we may also call in the service of the Nigerian Police Force."

Did he say suspended? She had exams tomorrow and for the rest of the week.

"Please, sir. You can't suspend me. I have my final exams to complete. I can explain everything."

"You can explain everything when you are invited to the disciplinary hearing. In the meantime, you are no longer permitted on the school premises. I will send a memo immediately informing all the affected lecturers."

"Dean Preye, would you mind if I have a talk with the young lady privately?" Telema said in a calm voice.

"Of course, Mr. George. I will excuse the two of you while I speak to my assistant." The man stood up and left the office, shutting the door behind him.

"You did this, didn't you?" Tessa rounded on Telema.

"Of course, I did. You didn't think you'd get away with insulting me over at Park Hotel the other time. I told you I'd get you. Here we are." He waved his hands in the air.

Tessa squeezed her eyes shut and counted to five. She wanted to strangle Telema and wipe the smile off his face. But she had to calm down. Perhaps if she grovelled, he would feel better with his ego.

"Look. I'm sorry. I panicked that night. I don't know. My head wasn't in the right place. And when you accused me of stealing, I just didn't want anything to do with you. I was worried about what else you would do if I went back to your room."

"All I wanted to do that night was to fuck you. I still want to fuck you." Telema traced the tip of his finger down her arm.

Her skin crawled and she tried not to pull back. "I'm not that girl anymore. I don't go to the club anymore. I'm not interested in doing that again."

"Yes, I noticed you stopped going to the club. I also noticed you are now hanging around with the owner of Park Hotel."

She reared back. "How did you know that?"

He shrugged. "I've had you followed. How do you think I found out about you? I paid someone to follow you and find out about you."

Oh God. She scrubbed a hand over her face. "You had me followed, which is just weird. I'm just a girl you met for one night. It doesn't make any sense."

"It might not to you. But no one ever says 'no' to me. I always get what I want and I want you."

She shoved back her chair and stood up. "And you're willing to ruin my life because you want me. Because I wouldn't have sex with you."

"I don't care. I do whatever I have to do to get what I want. All you have to do is come back with me and I will tell the dean to forget the allegations and reinstate you into the school. I will tell him it has all been a mistake."

Shit. She clenched her hands into fists. What was she going to do now? The exams were important. She needed to take them and get good scores to get a place at this university to do a full degree programme. And the exam tomorrow was one of the most important. If she didn't sit it and still sat the others, she wouldn't get entry.

It looked like she had no other option but to agree to have sex with Telema so he could call off this thing with the dean.

Even if she appealed, it would still take days—weeks—for her case to be heard and dealt with. In the meantime, she would miss out on her exams and would have to repeat the whole year.

Peter wasn't even back in the country to help her and Anuli wasn't talking to her.

What was she going to do?

Throw a whole year of studies away or have sex with a man who wasn't Peter?

She had been working on reclaiming what little dignity she had in the past few days. Giving in to Telema would be selling her body again, this time so she could stay in school.

Yes, she'd worked so hard for this school place. All the years of studying to get her GCEs and get enough to get an entry into the pre-degree programme. It had been her blood, sweat and tears. She'd sold her body to get money to pay for tutorials. She'd burned the candles at both ends just to make it through.

And now, it looked like she was going back to square one anyway.

Well, she was done letting men like Telema bully her and force her into doing something she didn't want.

"Do you know what, Mr. George," she spat out. "If you were the last man on Earth, I wouldn't have sex with you. Even if you paid me a million dollars. So, you can go to Hell and take the school with you."

She stormed out of the office, not even paying attention to the dean or his assistant. She kept her head high as she walked out of the school and got on a bike all the way back to the hotel.

It wasn't until she got into the quiet solitude of Peter's suite that it all dawned on her and she broke into tears, curled up on the sofa.

Everything she'd worked hard for over the last few years had just been lost.

Chapter Twenty-Three

"It's been a fun weekend getting together with the lads. But sometimes, I can't understand you guys," Paul said on the flight back from Barcelona.

He sat next to Peter in the first-class cabin. Michael sat on the other row, next to another friend of Paul's, Tunji.

"How do you mean?" Peter asked as he flicked through the in-flight magazine he had in his hands.

"Well, I understand Michael is taken with Kasie, although when they'll finally bite the bullet and set a wedding date, I don't know," Paul replied jovially.

"Yeah. He's still navigating his future in-laws. Considering the arrogance of the Bosas and the pomp and ceremony they will demand, which isn't Michael's thing, I don't blame him for being reluctant."

"You got that right."

"Actually, my money is on them eloping and getting married in secret and coming back to announce it to everyone."

"Thinking about it now, you could be correct. Michael is not averse to defying tradition. This brings me to you, Peter."

"What about me?" Peter quirked up his brow.

"Well, it's been five years since Naaza," Paul said in a sober tone that conveyed both his respect for Peter's late fiancée and his sympathy at her loss. "I know what she meant to you and I hope you don't misunderstand me. But you seemed so far away in Barcelona. It was as if you weren't even there half the time. You're never going to meet someone new if you won't even let any woman close. I was hoping you would loosen up but you were worse than everyone else."

Peter sighed. His friend had a valid point. All through the weekend, his thoughts had been consumed by Tessa. He'd joined in with most of the group activities. However, in the night clubs they'd visited, he hadn't interacted with any female company.

He'd kept thinking of Tessa and the first night they'd bumped into each other. The way they'd danced and him nearly taking her back to his suite. She'd eventually ended up in his suite under different circumstances. Now they were dating.

"I met someone," he said to his friend.

Paul made a show of slumping over in this chair. His expression was incredulous. "Say what?"

Peter rolled his eyes. "I said I met someone."

Paul pretended falling over again.

Michael leaned in their direction, having noticed his friend's antics. "What's going on over there?"

"Peter said he met someone." Paul had a huge grin on his face.

"He did. When? Where? How?" Michael rattled off.

"I'm getting the entire gist first." Paul called dibs.

"Then we're swapping places so I can hear the story too." Michael grinned.

Peter laughed. "The two of you are not serious."

"Come on, tell me. I want all the gory details." Paul rubbed his palms together. "What's her name? Where did you meet her and when do we get to meet this woman that snagged your attention?"

Paul chuckled as he answered the questions. "Her name is Tessa. I met her in Port Harcourt and you get to meet her at your traditional wedding."

He kept to the simple facts. Tessa had vowed not to work as a prostitute any longer and he saw no need to mention that to his friends. It would remain between him and her.

"Wow. This is serious. You're bringing her along to meet everyone at the same time, including your family. That's making a statement."

"You know me well enough to know that I don't do casual. But I like Tessa."

"Like?" Paul looked at her as if he didn't believe him.

"Okay. I care about her a lot. When I think of her, I think of all the things that are possible in my life. I think about having a life partner again and loving again. It's scary but it's freeing too. And the weird thing is that she is so different from Naaza and still there are similarities.

"Wow. I'm so happy to see you talking about someone. How about Tessa? How does she feel about you?"

He shrugged. "It's early days. But I think she cares about me. At least from what I've seen so far."

She'd made him so happy in the time they'd spent together after their weekend in Richa. It had been as if they were both new people. Just having her around as he'd worked on his laptop and she'd studied for her exams had been exhilarating.

They connected on a level beyond the physical. Even when he couldn't see her, just knowing she was close by relaxed him and put him in a great frame of mind.

He'd called her every night while he'd been in Barcelona. Now on the way back to Nigeria, he couldn't wait to see her again.

He knew she had exams this week and probably should leave her alone so she could concentrate on her papers.

But he wasn't sure he could last until the weekend to see her again.

"Well done, ol' boy. I really wish you the very best with Tessa," Paul said.

"Thank you," Peter replied. He really hoped for the best with her too.

As soon as he disembarked from the flight, she was the first person he called. The phone rang several times and wasn't picked up.

He assumed she was busy with studies and sent her a text message.

***

Hey countess, I called you but didn't get any response. You're probably revising so I won't disturb you. Just landed in MMA and catching the connecting flight to Enugu. Speak to you later tonight. xx

Tessa stared at the text message. She'd missed his call when she'd been curled up on the sofa crying. In her exhaustion from the tears, she'd fallen asleep on the sofa. She'd woken up to the sound of her phone beeping with a text message.

She rocked in place as she rolled her shoulders. What was she going to do about Peter? He had been so encouraging about her studies. He'd even called last night to wish her the best for today's exam.

When she spoke to him, he would surely ask how it went and if she was prepared for tomorrow. What would she tell him?

She couldn't lie to him. Yet, she couldn't tell him the truth. He would be disappointed and it would be another reason for him not to trust her. It would be the final straw for him to find out that she'd hidden her identity from him. He hated any form of deception.

Anuli was right. Her world would come crumbling down. It was best for her to go now. She would have to move again and relocate to a different city, now that her identity had been blown.

She couldn't afford for the man she was running from to find her. The police would come looking for her. She would be locked up. Imprisoned for what she'd done.

She couldn't get Peter involved in her mess. It would mess up his business with her bad reputation. After everything he'd done for her, she couldn't do that to him.

***

Peter arrived in Port Harcourt on Tuesday mid-morning and headed straight for a meeting with Christopher. He wasn't scheduled to be in PHC. But after he'd been unable to reach Tessa on either her phone or the hotel phones, he'd had to send Christopher up to the penthouse to check on Tessa. The man had returned with the news that Tessa wasn't in the suite.

He'd had a bad feeling about her and had driven down with his chauffeur as soon as he could get away from Enugu.

Now the manager confirmed Tessa hadn't spent the night in the hotel. He headed back out. She had exams today, so he'd go to her university and pick her up after her exams.

On the campus, he asked to see the Dean of the faculty and waited briefly before being ushered into the man's office.

He introduced himself and told the man the name of the student he'd come to see.

"Mr. Oranye, I'm afraid Ms. Obum is not permitted on the school premises until further notice," the dean said.

Peter jerked back. "Why? She's scheduled to have examinations this week."

"That was true but she is currently under investigation for registering as a student under fraudulent means and has been suspended."

Peter narrowed his eyes. "When did this happen?"

"Yesterday. I've already issued a memo to that effect. We are involving the police in the investigation."

No wonder Tessa didn't take his call yesterday. She had this to deal with.

"What exactly did she do?"

"She registered as a student with a false name and fake identity papers. We take such matters seriously."

Why would Tessa do such a thing?

He remembered the conversation he'd had with her about her father. She'd run away from home. Had she changed her name afterwards because of her past? It was possible if she didn't want to be found.

Why hadn't she told him this before now? He hated deception of any sort.

But then, how would the school find out such a thing if she'd already been studying here for the past year?

"I understand why you had to take punitive measures. Can I ask how you found out about the deception, Dean Preye?"

"One of our alumni informed me of the fraud and I took action immediately. Mr. George is a prominent member of the alumni community."

"Do you mean Telema George?" Peter asked.

"Yes. Do you know him?"

"I am acquainted with Mr. George," Peter said, trying not to grit his teeth. Telema would be getting very acquainted with him when he got his hands on the man.

Peter leaned forward in his chair. "Dean Preye, I believe you are a man of distinction and integrity. It is the reason I want to tell you something very confidential and I believe you will do the right thing."

"Yes, of course." The man preened. "You can talk to me in confidence."

"A few weeks ago, Mr. George attempted to rape Ms. Obum in my hotel. The girl was distressed and Mr. George wanted to take advantage of her. I investigated the matter and would've gotten the police involved but only changed my mind after Mr. George begged me to drop the matter. The girl indicated that the man was going to do something bad to her. But I didn't believe it until now."

"But that cannot be right," the dean said. "Telema is the son of a prominent citizen of the state. His father is highly regarded."

"And we know that sometimes, the apple falls far from the tree. Did you check Ms. Obum's current academic and attendance record? Is she a bad student? Have you had any problems with her before now?"

"Yes, I checked her record." The dean tugged at his shirt collar. "Ms. Obum has an excellent academic record and her attendance record is above average at ninety eight percent. We haven't had any problems with her beforehand."

"Compared to Mr. George, would you say Ms. Obum was a better student?"

He tugged his collar again as if he was getting hot and uncomfortable. "Well, I can't compare the two of them. Mr. George was a young man and they are usually more boisterous."

"So, you're saying his academic record wasn't impeccable yet you took his words over that of an above-average student with an impeccable record. This is quite a biased approach, don't you think? Since Ms. Obum is my fiancée, I will be advising my lawyers to take immediate action against you and this university."

Peter hoped he wasn't a dean who would drag his faculty and reputation into the mud of a lawsuit.

Mr. Preye spluttered. "Erm. Hold on a minute. There's no need for that. Anyway, I took the information on good faith."

"And I'm telling you in good faith. Ms. Obum is an upstanding citizen. You can go and check out my credentials. I can vouch for the young lady."

"Of course, if you will vouch for her, then I will take your word for it."

"Then reinstate her immediately and see to it that she takes any exams that she's already missed out on."

"Yes, I will do that right away."

"Good. I'll wait for the reinstatement letter. In the meantime, excuse me while I make a call."

Peter stepped outside the dean's office and called Tessa's number for what seemed like the hundredth time today, hoping she would pick it this time.

Chapter Twenty-Four

Tears rolled down Tessa's face as she packed the last of her things into a suitcase. She didn't have many things and had only acquired a lot of clothes in the past few weeks on the two shopping trips instigated by Peter.

Just when she thought something good was happening in her life, everything had gone wrong.

She'd lost her best friend whom she hadn't seen for a few days now, and she was running away again which was effectively ending her relationship with Peter.

She was going to have to leave the two most important people in her life and walk the road alone. At least when she'd run away from home the last time, she'd had Anuli. Now she would have to do it on her own.

The alternative was unthinkable. Getting arrested and going to jail. And dragging Peter down in the process.

No. She couldn't do it.

Ideally, Anuli should get out of here too. But since she hadn't seen her friend, she'd written a note telling her what happened in the Dean's office.

Anuli had always been able to take care of herself and she'd be alright without Tessa.

Tessa zipped up the suitcase and stood it upright beside the door. She'd only taken her personal things. She'd left the items that she shared with Anuli like the cooking utensils, plates and so on. She would buy new ones when she arrived wherever she was going.

She didn't even have a destination in mind. Just anywhere she wasn't likely to bump into anyone from her past. She'd thought about heading to Calabar and perhaps acquiring a passport so she could travel to Cameroon. She had been studying French and could read and write it. If she'd taken the exams today and passed, she was hoping to get a place to study Languages with French as a major.

She looked around the room one last time. The last time she'd run away, she'd left home with just a backpack and had left a room full of luxury items and bad memories. This time, she stared at a room filled with basic items but good memories.

No matter what had happened between her and Anuli in recent days, she would always be grateful to Anuli for being her anchor for so long.

In the past few weeks, Peter had become her anchor. Her solid rock. She was going to miss him. She slumped on the chair, put her head and arms on the desk and sobbed again.

"Tessa! Tessa!"

She lifted her head at the sound of someone calling her name and swiped her face with her hands.

Anuli barged into the room. "Tessa..."

The other girl stopped as soon as she saw Tessa. "What's going on?"

Tessa shrugged, unable to work words into her dry mouth.

"I came out of my exams only for one of the girls to tell me that you've been suspended. I didn't believe her. I went around the whole school looking for you."

Tessa turned around as she inhaled deeply. "Yes. The dean suspended me. Telema George found out about the fake ID and reported me to the dean. I'm not allowed on the school premises. Anyway, it doesn't matter. I'm leaving Port Harcourt."

"What? You're running away?" Anuli looked flabbergasted.

"Yes, what else can I do? Telema knows about our IDs. How long before the investigation digs up more and what we did gets exposed? You know what will happen once the police get involved."

"Shit. I know. I know." Anuli scrubbed a hand over her head. "Why didn't you tell me all this?"

"Because you're not taking my calls. Anyway, I thought you might be able to get away with it. Telema wasn't after you. He was after me. So, you can still finish your exams and get your results. At least this whole year won't be wasted for you like it is for me."

"I swear if I get my hands on that Telema, I'll—"

"No. Anuli. No more. We're in enough trouble as it is. Let's not add to it. You stay in Port Harcourt. I will send you a message when I get to where I'm going so you know I'm okay."

"Tessa, you don't have to go—"

"No, I do." Tessa choked. "I can't bear to drag Peter into my shit. He's such a good man. He doesn't deserve the mess that is my life."

Anuli gripped her shoulders. "Tessa, listen to me. You don't have to go. You're right. Peter is a great man."

"What are you talking about?" Tessa's mouth dropped open.

"Just hold on." Anuli pulled a brown envelope out of her bag and held it out. "Go on. Open it."

Tessa took the item from Anuli. It had her name on it. Tentatively, she ripped it open and pulled out the sheet of paper inside. A letter from the dean reinstating her in school and apologising for the misunderstanding. She was also invited to sit the paper she had missed today on a different date.

She couldn't believe it. She rubbed her eyes and read it again.

"How did this happen? Why did the dean change his mind? Did you do this?" The questions hurtled from her lips as her body trembled with shock.

"It wasn't me." Anuli shook her head. "The person who did it for you is standing on the other side of the door. And it is clear to me that he loves you as much as I love you. Perhaps more than I love you. So, if you're going to run away, I suggest you run to him, babe."

There was only one person Tessa could think about. "Peter?"

Anuli nodded with a smile.

"He's here?"

"Yes, babe. I went to the dean's office to find out for sure and found him there with this letter in his hand. He'd already spoken to the dean and got it all sorted."

Tears filled Tessa's eyes and dropped down her face. "But how did he know? He's supposed to be in Enugu."

"Babe, you're going to have to speak to him and find out. I'm going next door to give you guys some space to talk. After what he's just done for you, you have my permission to tell him the truth about everything."

Anuli leaned in and brushed her lips on Tessa's cheek before opening the door and stepping out.

Two seconds later, Peter filled the door frame with his powerful presence. He was looking at her with a deep sadness in his eyes.

Her heart raced and she licked her lips, unable to speak. She hadn't seen him in about a week and he seemed larger than life.

"Were you really planning on running away?" he asked in a sober tone.

She lowered her gaze, suddenly fascinated with the bare cement floor. "Yes."

"And you weren't going to tell me." He said it as a statement as he took a step into the now cramped room.

She nodded as a tear rolled down. "I'm sorry."

He pulled in a deep breath. "It seems it's the curse of my life. To fall in love and to have the woman leave me. Naaza by death and you by running away."

She tilted her head back sharply, her eyes wide. Did she hear him correct? Did he just say he was in love with her? He couldn't love her. Who was she? A call girl with a dodgy past. She was so unsuitable for him, even if she loved him in return.

"So where are you running to?" He glanced around the room as he stepped further in and shut the door.

She felt rooted to the spot. "I was going to Calabar and perhaps Cameroon eventually." She couldn't lie to him about the things she'd thought about.

He nodded. "Calabar is very nice. You'll enjoy living there. Douala in Cameroon is one of our flight destinations. We're planning to expand our routes to Yaoundé also. So good choices."

"Peter..." she trailed off, not knowing what to say.

He was being very civil, not shouting at her like she expected. But Peter wasn't like other men. He always surprised her with his actions.

"Tell me one thing though. I mean, I can understand the reason you ran away from home. I can even understand you changing your identity so that you wouldn't be found in case your father and his friends were looking for you. But you're an adult now. They can't do anything to you now. And the university already did its worst by suspending you. They couldn't do much else. So why run away again? Why leave your friend who has been with you for years? Never mind me."

Tessa slumped into the chair, all her energy drained. When he put it like that, it looked simple but it wasn't.

"I was running away because I didn't want to have the police involved. I didn't want to drag you into the subsequent mess."

He lowered his body onto the mattress, sitting to face her, his elbows on his knees. "I'm a big boy. I can handle the police and I won't let them touch you anyway."

She turned her face away. "You won't be able to save me from this."

He reached across and dragged her up. "Sit beside me and tell me what's eating you up inside, Tessa. Tell me the reason you were willing to break my heart. I've been trying to contact you since yesterday. I left my business and everything else I should be doing to come to Port Harcourt today to find out what was going on. I dealt with the issue of your fake ID and solved the problem with the school. The least you can do is to tell me the goddamn truth."

Oh God. She covered her face with her hands as more tears rushed out. "The truth is that when we left Okigwe, Anuli and I didn't just run away. We killed my father."

Chapter Twenty-Five

Seven years ago

"Hurry up!"

The sound of urgency in her friend's voice only made Tessa's hands shake violently as she stuffed clothes and other items into a small backpack.

Anuli, the only person she could refer to as friend these days, stood by the door keeping watch and listening out.

Clothes littered the room, bed and floor. Usually, Tessa would never allow her personal space to be in such disarray but she didn't have the time to tidy up right now. It was more important that she packed up and got out of this house as soon as possible.

Her gaze swept over the walls and furniture quickly as she tried to make sure she'd taken the things that were important to her. She had many beautiful things, clothes, gifts, ornaments, more than a normal girl of sixteen would own in a country like Nigeria.

But she wasn't normal. And the gifts had been from her father.

"Am I really doing the right thing?" Tessa asked, her tight grip on the rucksack handle making it cut into her palm.

"Of course, you are," Anuli replied with a quick glance over her left shoulder. "We discussed this, didn't we? You can't go to the police. You tried that already."

Tessa bit the inside of her lower lip. Yes, she'd gone to the police and no one had believed her claim. Her stomach tightened and she struggled not to be sick as she sat on the edge of the bed. "I know we did. But running away to Port Harcourt?"

She lived in the small town of Okigwe. It was nothing more than a dusty motorway town that happened to have a university on its periphery. It wasn't the most exciting place in the world but it was all that she knew.

"We both need to get as far away as possible from here." Anuli came over, sat beside Tessa on the edge of the bed and took her hand. "We have two options—head north to Enugu or south to Port Harcourt. We don't know anyone in Enugu but I have a distant Aunt in PHC that we could stay with, hopefully. We talked about this already."

Her friend squeezed her hand. Tessa sucked in a deep breath and swallowed hard before nodding. Running away would create its own problems, but anywhere else had to be better than the nightmare of the gilded cage she currently lived in.

She closed her eyes and the horror assaulted her—hot sweaty hands, the press of suffocating weight on top of her, the cloying body musk. Her skin tightened as if she had thousands of ants crawling over it and her eyes flew open.

Fighting nausea, she jumped off the bed and snatched her backpack. "We need to go now."

She couldn't bear to look at the items without distaste. They had only been items locking her into the horror that was her life. She could afford to leave them all here. But she would need her phone, so she grabbed it. And she also took out the cash she'd hidden away and stuffed it into the backpack.

She took one last look at the space before saying, "I'm ready to go."

Tessa rushed out of the room, not giving it another glance as Anuli followed her.

"Come on, then," Anuli said and led the way out of the room. She couldn't bear to be in this house anymore. Not another night. Not another moment. She barely breathed as they raced down the stairs. The thudding of their shoes against the concrete seemed to match the thumping of heartbeats.

They descended halfway when the front door swung open. The hairs on her nape and arms lifted as she froze on the spot.

Tessa's father walked in. He was dressed in the flamboyant lace up and down he favoured. He was a wealthy man and owned several properties in the town. A man that a lot of people respected outside. If only they knew what he did in his home.

Tessa's first impulse was to rush down to greet him as per usual. But Anuli held her arm, stopping her.

"Welcome home, Daddy,"

The man looked up and saw them. First, he had a smile which soon disappeared. "Mary Theresa, I've told you not to have people in the house when I'm not here."

Tessa swallowed as her heart thumped. Her father always addressed her with her full name when he was reprimanding her, although everyone knew her as Mary.

"Sir, you know who I am and I'm not a stranger." Her friend stepped down, carrying Tessa's backpack.

The man stared at her then back to Tessa and shook his head, his expression angry.

"Does Joe know you're here? I've warned him to keep you two separated. I don't like having you two together when no one else is here. You are a bad influence on my daughter. You make her reject my gifts and turn against me. Hang on. That is Mary's bag you're carrying."

Tessa knew she had to speak up. "Yes, it's my bag. I'm leaving."

The man flinched as if she'd slapped him. "You're leaving? Why?"

"Because of what you do to me. It's wrong and it needs to stop."

"How can it be wrong?" His voice softened. "I love you and I take care of you. I buy you beautiful gifts more than any girl in this town ever gets. What father loves his daughter the way I love you?"

"Your love is sick," Anuli shouted. "And she needs to get away from you."

Her father backhanded Anuli. She staggered backward. He followed her and kept punching. "I see that Joe hasn't taught you to behave. In this house, girls are seen not heard. I will teach you that lesson."

"Stop!" Tessa shouted, afraid her father would kill Anuli. She grabbed the bronze statue at the bottom of the stairs and hit him over the head. He slumped onto the ground. The object clattered onto the floor as she rushed to pull Anuli up. "I'm so sorry."

"It's okay. I'm alright," Anuli said and swiped at the cut on her lip. Her finger came away bloody.

Tessa rushed to the kitchen to get the first aid kit. She would take care of Anuli and then her father who seemed to have passed out and then they would get out of here. There was no way she could stay here now that she'd hit the man.

The man would get Anuli arrested and Tessa's misery would only double.

She pulled out the square box just as Anuli rushed in. "Your father is dead. We need to get out of here now."

"What? He's not dead. He can't be," Tessa said and rushed out of the kitchen.

"You hit him very hard. He's not breathing and there's blood all over the floor and the walls."

"No!" Tessa covered her mouth at the gore in front of her. Her stomach churned and she bent over and puked all over the floor.

She was in a state of shock as Anuli dragged her back into the kitchen and cleaned her up. Then she dragged Tessa out of the house.

Tessa was still numb as they both walked down the street and flagged down an okada motorbike. They got on and were far away when Tessa chanced one last look in the direction of her house. She could never return to that house now as the police would soon be looking for them.

Chapter Twenty-Six

"What the hell!" Peter shouted, leapt off the bed and began pacing the small room in an agitated manner.

Tessa had never seen him this angry. His whole body was wound tight and he looked like he would punch something.

"You have to believe me. It was self-defence. I hit him only because of the way he was beating Anuli. He was furious with her. With both of us because I said I was leaving." Tessa clutched her arms around her stomach, pleading for him to understand why they'd done what they did.

She hadn't set out to kill her father. Just to get away from him. Afterwards, they'd had no option but to run away, afraid of what would happen to them if they'd stayed.

Peter froze and swivelled to face her. Then he came back and sat on the bed beside her. His lips twisted in agony as the corners of his eyes pinched.

"Of course, I believe you, Tessa. I'm just devastated that you had to go through all that to escape the nightmare of your father's abuse. No one should have to endure what you endured. And it breaks my heart to see you so upset about it."

He pulled her into a hug and held her for a long time. This man continued to surprise her. To uplift her and she really didn't know how else to thank him or to show her gratitude.

"Peter." She pulled back so she could look into his eyes. "The decision for me to run away this time was not an easy one. It tore me up. But I only decided because I didn't want you to see me as a murderer as well as call girl. And the fact that I love you means I don't want your life to become messed up when this whole thing blows up."

His lips tugged up at the corners. "Okay. First things first. Did you just say that you love me?"

She lowered her gaze, suddenly feeling self-conscious. She hadn't been aware when she'd used the words 'I love you'. But they had been the truth.

"Yes, Peter. I love you."

His knuckles pushed her chin up and he gazed into her eyes with a face lit up in a smile that sent warmth across her chest.

"Oh countess, that's the best thing I've heard all day because I love you too."

"You do?" She blinked rapidly as a lump formed in her throat. "Even after everything I've just told you?"

"I do. I love you more knowing what you've endured. I love your spirit and your resilience. I love the fighter in you. I could go on all day listing all the things I love about you."

She placed her head on his chest, clutching him tight. "How did I get so lucky? How did I manage to get you into my life?"

"I think I got lucky when you stumbled right out of the ladies' into me. You changed my life that night."

She leaned back to look up at him. "*I* changed your life?"

He was grinning. "Yes, you gave me a new lease of life. My life hasn't been the same since. This is why you must stay in my life. I can't lose you, Tessa. I can't go back to the broken heart and empty existence without you."

"But what am I going to do if the police turn up and start asking questions?"

He grabbed her hands and held them together in his. "You don't have to face them alone. You have me and I know people. Including the attorney general of the country. I promise you that I will make those men pay for what they did to you and Anuli."

"You do?"

"Yes. So, here's what I want to suggest. Instead of sitting down and waiting for the police to show up, I want to start an investigation to find out what happened after you girls left Okigwe. I also want to investigate your father's friend Uncle Joe and find out if he's still alive. I want to find out all I can about the men who molested you girls and bring them to justice. Men like that are predators and there's a strong likelihood he is still preying on other girls."

"Oh God." Tessa covered her face with her hands. "You're right. We were so focused on getting away that we didn't even want to think about

Uncle Joe. He's probably found other girls to rape and enslave just like he did Anuli."

Nausea rose in her gut at the idea of any number of girls been molested by the man and his group of paedophiles.

"This is why I think you and Anuli should stop running. You are both strong girls and you've survived this. You could be a beacon of hope and inspiration to other children out there who are going through similar things."

Her hands trembled. "You're right, Peter. I've spent so long running and hiding. If I can help anyone else out, I'd like to."

"So, you'll stay?"

"Yes, Peter. I'll stay."

He puffed out breath as if in relief. "I'm so glad to hear that Tessa. I'm going to be with you every step of the way from now on. There's something I have to tell you about the night we spent in Richa Ranch."

She closed her eyes as heat flushed her cheeks. She'd tried to forget that night. "What?"

"Look at me." He spoke in a soft voice.

She lifted her gaze to him.

"The man who spent the night with you— Master Chi—that was me."

"You?" She shook her head. "It can't be. It didn't sound like you. He was dominant. Forceful."

"I put on the accent to disguise my voice. As for being dominant, that was me. Naaza and I discovered the place many years ago when we were exploring our sexuality and trying out new things. That side of me lay dormant for years because I didn't know I would find another woman who pushed my buttons that way. You do."

Her cheeks heated again at some of the sex they'd had that night. He'd indeed been fierce at times. "But why would you... you were harsh."

"The purpose of the evening was to punish you. There was no way I would allow anyone else to touch you. So, I asked Sir Melaye to bid on my behalf. With the blindfold on you, I could become Master Chi for the night."

She nodded. "I understand. I deserved the punishment. But I'm glad it was you and not somebody else."

"Good. So, let's get you packed up. You're moving into the suite with me and as soon as you finish your exams and can get away, you're coming up to Enugu and staying with me until this is all sorted out."

"Are you sure? You do realise that there's a strong chance that I'll go to prison for murder."

"For starters, if your father is dead, then it is manslaughter by way of self-defence due to extenuating circumstances. A very good lawyer should be able to get an acquittal in court."

"But I might still get locked up."

"This is the reason I want to spend all the available time together while we work this all out. On the other hand, your father could still be alive. You have no real proof of his death."

She frowned. Could her father really be alive? After all these years? The last time she'd seen him, he hadn't been breathing and there'd been blood everywhere.

"He has to be dead. Otherwise, he would have found us. He had the money to do so and the police were in his pocket."

"Anyway, let's forget your father for now. What matters now is that I love you, Countess, and I'll be here for you no matter what happens."

When he called her countess, he made her heart sing. She leaned in and pressed her lips against his.

"You are a godsend, Peter. My rock. You brought light into my dark world and showed me love like no other man ever did. I love you, today, tomorrow and forever."

He took her lips in a kiss filled with the passion and promise of forever.

Epilogue

"Are you ready?" Peter called out from his living room to Tessa.

"Just a minute," Tessa replied from the bedroom where she was getting dressed.

They were in his apartment in Enugu and would be heading out shortly to Paul's house. Today was Paul's traditional wedding to Ijay which would be happening in Ijay's hometown. Peter and Michael were part of Paul's entourage so they would travel with Paul and his relatives in a convoy to the venue.

It was only seven in the morning. All the preparations for the occasion had been done. Peter wanted to be at his friend's side in case there was an emergency that needed dealing with. But Tessa was coming with him and as she didn't know anyone else very well, he didn't want to leave her to travel to the event separately.

The past few weeks with Tessa had been amazing. He hadn't believed he'd be happy again with a woman after Naaza. But he'd been proven wrong. He'd finally laid Naaza's ghost to rest and made peace with himself.

Now, he was focused on building a life with Tessa. First, they had to deal with the obstacles ahead which included arresting the man known as Uncle Joe and prosecuting him and anyone else involved in the paedophilia ring.

On a positive note, they'd found Tessa's father. Apparently, the injury to his head hadn't killed him but the man had been left paralysed and almost destitute.

Tessa had cried with relief at the news but she hadn't wanted to see the man again. Peter couldn't blame her. At least now, she was free of the worry of being arrested.

He heard the click of footsteps in the hallway and turned around as Tessa entered the living room. His breath caught in his throat and warmth spread across his chest.

She was unrecognisable from the vampy bombshell he'd bumped into months ago in Port Harcourt. There was none of that girl evident in the woman that stood before him now. Gone were the hair extensions, provocative clothes and makeup.

Tessa looked stunning in the plum and pink Ankara print dress and the plum velvet high-heeled sandals that just begged him to fuck her.

Before he knew what he was doing, he'd demolished the space between them and tugged her into his arms. He tucked hair behind her ear and kissed a path down her neck.

"What are you doing?" she asked in a breathy voice.

"You are so damned irresistible." He sealed their lips together, licking her strawberry-flavoured lip gloss as he ravaged her mouth. His arousal flared, his erection pulsing with each rapid beat of his heart.

He broke the kiss, panting. "I need to be inside you."

He cupped her left breast, pinched the nipple through the fabric of her dress and bra.

"Oh God. Yes," she moaned, arching her body into his touch.

Releasing her breast, he spun her around and shoved her onto the back of the sofa. "Bend over."

She gave him a sultry smile as she complied, pulling her dress up over her hips. She spread her legs, giving him a view of her bare chocolate bum cheeks not concealed by the tiny scrap of material that claimed to be underwear. One of the things he loved about her, this boldness of hers that defied convention.

His heart felt as if he would explode in his chest and he could likely come just from the sight of her like this. They'd made love earlier before showering to get dressed. Perhaps it was the years of not having sex and his body was trying to catch up. He was insatiable when it came to Tessa.

"Peter, aren't we going to be late?" she asked but the expression on her face said she didn't want to move until they were both sated. She braced her hands on the top of the sofa and lowered her upper body, pushing out her bum more.

"We have time," he replied as he went down on his knees. He would worry about tidying up his clothes later.

Pushing the thong aside, he traced his index finger along the seam of her pussy. His fingers slid along the slick, dewy pink flesh.

"Oh," she mewled, rocking her hips.

Dipping his head, he parted her brown labia, revealing the pink clit. He captured the bud in his mouth, her tang filling him as he rolled his tongue over it before sucking.

"Oh... Oh." Her thighs trembled as she rocked into him.

He loved the sounds she made her as well as the taste of her in his mouth. He thrust two fingers inside her hot, wet channel and she clamped around his digits as he pumped in rhythm to her movements.

Her insides fluttered around his fingers just as her rocking became erratic. He sucked hard on her clip as she detonated in climax.

"Peter!" His name on her lips was both supplication and praise.

He stood, unzipped his trousers and pulled out his cock. Left hand on her hip, he guided his shaft to her dripping entrance with his right hand. With a slam, he was fully encased in her wet heat.

"*Countess.*" The word ripped out of his hoarse throat. He stood still, took shallow breaths to quell an impending orgasm. He didn't want to come too quickly. Being inside her drove him out of control. He withdrew halfway and thrust back in. And did this again and again. Slowly.

"Peter, please harder." She turned her head and gave him the lusty expression that heated his blood.

All at once, he lost control. Gripping her hips, he slammed in and out of her as hard as she wanted. Soon, the slap of flesh against flesh mixed with their moans and groans.

As she rippled around him in orgasm, his climax hit him with full force. He rammed in, releasing his seed inside her. They'd talked about babies. He was ready. She said she was ready too. Maybe soon, they'd make one. Maybe today.

He pulled out of her, turned her around and kissed her as emotions swelled inside him. He couldn't believe he could be lucky to find love twice in his life.

Later, after they'd cleaned and tidied their appearances, they sat in the back seats of the car on the way to Paul's house.

Tessa fidgeted with her purse and he placed his hand over hers to still it.

"You have to stop fidgeting," he said in a low voice.

"I'm nervous. I've never done anything like this before," she said in a shaky voice.

He turned to look at her, his brows pulled together. "You haven't been to a wedding before?"

She glanced at him and looked away at the scenery past the window. "No."

He squeezed her hand. "You'll be fine. You met Paul, Michael, Ijay and Kasie at the pre-wedding dinner, so you'll be fine."

"I know. They are all lovely and nice. But I'm worried about your parents. I get to meet them today for the first time."

"My parents are the easiest going parents. I promise you. You have nothing to worry about." He lifted her hand and brushed his lips against the back of it.

She beamed a smile at him and leaned across to kiss him briefly. "I love you, Peter. Thank you for giving me a new life."

"I should thank you, Countess. You revitalised my life. And I look forward to spending the rest of my life with you."

He reached inside his pocket and pulled out the small box. "I wanted to wait until later today to do this. I didn't want to detract from Paul's day. But this has been burning a hole in my pocket and I really can't wait any longer."

He opened the box, revealing a diamond-set-in-gold ring.

Tessa gasped, eyes wide, hand on chest. "Is that what I think it is?"

She glanced from the ring to Peter's face.

"Yes." A smile broke on his face. "I love you and you know I want to spend the rest of my life with you. Please do me the honour of being my wife."

Her eyes went glassy and she hiccupped before blinking a few times. She met his gaze as a smile bloomed across her face. "Yes, Peter. I will be your wife."

He exhaled in relief as he slid the ring onto her finger and kissed her passionately.

Dear Reader,

Thank you for reading Worthy. If you enjoyed this story, please leave a quick review on the site of purchase.

There next story in the Challenge series is out now and features Anuli, Tessa's friend, and Tope, Peter's chief of security.

I offer my mailing list subscribers the chance to read previews of upcoming books before the release date. Make sure you don't miss out on the free reads, giveaways and news of upcoming book events by visiting my website www.kirutaye.com and signing up for my mailing list.

Until our next fictional adventure,
Kiru xx